GHOST MARKET

Books by Angela Roquet

Lana Harvey, Reapers Inc.
Graveyard Shift
Pocket Full of Posies
For the Birds
Psychopomp
Death Wish
Ghost Market
Hellfire and Brimstone
Limbo City Lights (short story collection)
The Illustrated Guide to Limbo City

Return to Limbo City (A Lana Harvey Spin-off Series)
Life After Death
Shadow of Death

Blood Vice
Blood Vice
Blood and Thunder
Blood in the Water
Blood Dolls
Thicker Than Blood
Blood, Sweat, and Tears
Flesh and Blood
Out for Blood

Spero Heights
Blood Moon
Death at First Sight
The Midnight District

Haunted Properties: Magic and Mayhem Universe
How to Sell a Haunted House
Better Haunts and Graveyards
This Old Haunt

Visit **angelaroquet.com** for a complete list of Angela's works.

GHOST MARKET

LANA HARVEY, REAPERS INC.

BOOK SIX

ANGELA ROQUET

VIOLENT SIREN PRESS

GHOST MARKET

Copyright © 2016 by Angela Roquet

www.angelaroquet.com

Cover Art by Rebecca Frank

Edited by Chelle Olson of Literally Addicted to Detail

ISBN: 978-1-951603-07-6

For Paul. Again.
I know a lot of authors who dedicate their books to the same person over and over. Through the years, I've tried to spread the love around. I'm breaking habit and dedicating this one to my husband again. He deserves it, and so much more, for taking care of our son, our home, and me, day in and day out. None of what I do would be possible without his support, encouragement, and crazy good love.

♥

CHAPTER ONE

"A vacation is what you take when you can no longer take what you've been taking."
—Earl Wilson

A warm, furry body nuzzled under my arm, and the smell of wet dog assaulted me as I woke. Saul licked my ear, his muzzle grazing my cheek when the houseboat rocked, and even though I groaned in protest, a smile curled up one corner of my mouth. I rubbed my face dry on the wool blanket.

Beelzebub's muffled singing drifted down from the upper deck, accompanied by a gurgling hiss. A moment later, I smelled espresso. It motivated me to finally crack my eyes open. I blinked a few times, adjusting to the light that spilled past the gauzy curtains hanging over the small window of the lower cabin.

Saul's tail wagged, and his tongue slipped out for another kiss, but I pushed him away.

"I'm up. Okay? See?" I rolled off the bed, taking the blanket with me and accidentally knocking my hound to the floor. He jumped to his feet with a yap and raced up the cabin stairs to the main deck.

I followed him, emerging to find Bub standing stark naked at the helm, a cup of steaming coffee in hand. Scars wrapped around his left calf in a marbled pattern, but the round smoothness of his ass was unmarred. His black hair ran past the nape of his neck, grazing the tops of his shoulders. I grinned at the faint lines my fingernails had left there the night before.

The morning sky was bright orange, streaked through with wispy gray clouds. They reflected across the muddy waters of the Styx and repeated into the distance, hiding the peaks of the mountains that served as the backdrop of Bub's Tartarus property. The crew of trolls he'd hired to rebuild his summer home had almost finished with the stonework, and our afternoon plans included taking a peek at the progress.

Bub turned to greet me as I walked across the deck, letting his steering hand slip from the wheel to wrap around my waist. He pulled our hips together, leaving only the thin blanket between us.

"Good morning, my love, my dark queen of the night, my—"

"Drinker of coffee," I injected, nodding at the cup in his hand.

Bub snorted and tilted it to my lips. I closed my eyes and took a long drink, moaning my thanks. When I'd had my fill, he slowly pulled the cup back to his own mouth, darting his forked tongue out to lick a smear of coffee from the side that I'd drunk from. The gold flecks in his eyes swirled with lust. It was a look I knew all too well.

The wool blanket slipped from my naked shoulder, sending a shiver through me. Bub dropped the coffee mug to the deck floor and ran his hand through my tangled curls, dragging my face to his. Our mouths met savagely, tongues and teeth taking purchase wherever they could. Bub's other hand left my hip to claw at the hem of the blanket, tugging it down the length of my back until it fell to my feet.

I laced my fingers behind his neck and pulled him in closer. My breasts flattened against his chest, aching blissfully as his hands groped my body. I was dizzy with need and ready to take him right there at the helm. So, when a throat cleared at the opposite end of the deck, all I could manage was a vicious growl.

Saul let out a startled yap, and Bub jerked away from me, nearly losing his balance as he turned to face the unwelcome arrival. A small cluster of flies swarmed around his head as if he were on the verge of dispersing to attack.

Our *guest*, an armor-clad member of the Nephilim Guard, stood at attention with his spear crossed over his breastplate. I couldn't tell if the wideness of his eyes was more out of fear or embarrassment.

"Greetings and apologies, Captain Harvey. I am here to deliver an urgent message from President Fang. She requires your advisement on a sensitive matter. You are to report to her at Afterlife Council headquarters at once." The guard finished with a stiff bow and took flight, fleeing the houseboat as suddenly as he'd arrived.

"A sensitive matter?" Bub's lips pursed thoughtfully.

I scoffed. "President Fang? This promotion is going to her head." I nuzzled against Bub, but he leaned away to look down at me.

"We should probably head back to the city," he said. I gave him a sour look as he kissed the tip of my nose. "We'll pick up where we left off tonight—provided the world isn't coming to an end."

I rolled my eyes. "Fine."

My feet tripped over the abandoned wool blanket, and I stooped to pick it up, yelping when Bub's hand squeezed my backside.

"A little forget-me-not," he said with a chuckle.

I tossed my hair back and cocked an eyebrow at him as I headed for the cabin stairs.

Jenni had better be up to her eyeballs in some hellish wrath. Otherwise, she'd be getting an earful. At the same time, I really hoped that hellish wrath had a quick and easy solution.

This vacation was going too well to be cut short.

CHAPTER TWO

"If I had my choice I would kill every reporter in the world,
but I am sure we would be getting reports from Hell
before breakfast."
—William Tecumseh Sherman

The rest of the ride down the Styx was depressing. After I'd put on a pair of jeans and a tee shirt, I took Bub's place at the wheel so he could dress, too. I hadn't packed anything business-casual, but Jenni's message seemed urgent, so I wouldn't be making time to run home and change.

My agitation grew as Bub tied up the houseboat near the gates of Hell. By the time we coined off to go our separate ways, I was drowning in a stew of anxious irritation. Seriously, what was so damned important that it couldn't wait until Monday?

Limbo City's restricted coin travel landed all incoming traffic on the main dock pier at the harbor. It was quiet when I arrived, which I expected with most reapers off harvesting at this time of day. What did surprise me was the abandoned market area. It was Saturday morning. The Three Fates Factory employees were off work and should have been swarming the place.

Abe, the nephilim guarding the dock entrance, nodded stiffly as Saul and I passed by. He hadn't spared me much more than that since last fall when I gave him the slip while he was supposed to be babysitting me for Grim. I didn't hold it against him, but I still gave him a wide berth, remembering the time Loki had tricked me by taking on the guard's face.

From the sidewalk beyond the dock, I noticed half the tented booths down Market Street were closed, their tables tucked inside, the curtains drawn. A warm breeze pushed a paper coffee cup across the asphalt until it found the gutter, joining an assortment of crumpled receipts, candy wrappers, and cigarette butts. Saul lifted his nose to sniff the air and whimpered softly.

On the opposite side of the street, a yellow taxi was parked along the curb. I caught a glimpse of Skipper, the troll who owned the only cab business in Limbo, cramming an entire donut into his mouth.

The travel booths were faster and cheaper, so Skipper's business had taken a beating after the big transition. The nephilim driver he'd employed had joined the Guard, and his tree spirit cabbie had to take on a second job waiting tables at the Phantom Café.

I tapped on the window, giving Skipper a start. He swallowed hard as he pushed the button to unlock the back door.

"Didn't see you there," he said, rubbing his sleeve across his wide face. His voice was rough and soft at the same time, and it never failed to remind me of Batman.

"Got time for a fare to Reapers Inc.?" I asked, sliding across the back seat. Saul hopped in next to me, taking care to keep his clawed toes from injuring the upholstery.

"Kid, I got nothin' but time," Skipper said. He pushed a beefy finger down on the meter button and glanced at his side mirrors before pulling away from the curb.

As we turned left onto Morte Avenue, I realized the market wasn't the only part of the city suffering a lack of activity. Half the store windows were dark—even Purgatory Lounge, which was usually open by now for the early lunch crowd. I spotted a minor Roman god and a nephilim as they exited Bank of Eternity, but that was it.

"Did I overlook a big holiday, Skip?" I pressed my face against the window as we passed Destiny Avenue, trying to catch a glimpse of the city park, where the souls gathered to celebrate on occasion.

"I don't think so." Skipper sighed and handed me a magazine over his shoulder. It was the newest edition of *Limbo's Laundry*, the gossip rag that had shit on my name more times than I cared to count.

"You don't strike me as the kind of guy who reads trash talk." I made eye contact with Skipper in his rearview mirror and frowned at him.

He shrugged. "*Limbo Weekly* won't be out until Wednesday, and *The Reaper Report* didn't say much about it."

"About what?"

"The soul scare," he said, turning right on Ghost Alley.

I looked down at the magazine and crinkled my nose in disgust. The lead story was about the new soul organization, the Apparition Agency, headed up by Naledi, the soul on the Throne of Eternity. Bold text read: *Have the inmates taken over the asylum?*

Several of the Afterlife Council subcommittees weren't fully on board with the new addition, and with Grim missing in action and Jenni Fang having only just filled his shoes, the power struggle was getting intense. I was more than happy to pass when the reins were held in my direction, and I felt better about that decision every day.

Next to the tacky cover story, a sidebar of smaller photos and captions caught my attention. Gabriel and Amy's on-again, off-again romance was showcased between a speculation piece on whether or not Seth was alive and an article about several souls going missing in the past week. Folks didn't read *Limbo's Laundry* for the publication's ability to prioritize important issues.

I flipped the magazine open to the directory and found the listing for the soul article. Somehow, I wasn't surprised to see that it only warranted a single page. They'd even squeezed in an ad for overpriced protection amulets that readers could order directly from the magazine, of course.

I rolled my eyes and skimmed the article, looking for the bits that weren't just sensational fluff. A *"noticeable spike in CNH souls"* could mean anything from two to two hundred, so I refused to let the vague comment concern me just yet, though I was bothered by the mention of three factory souls disappearing.

Souls in the city didn't just disappear. The travel restrictions made that impossible. Unless they somehow slipped past the guards at the harbor and boarded a boat, they had to be somewhere in the city. The article went on to propose that they had grown sick of factory work and had run away, refusing to fulfill the century term of their contracts with the Fates. It was a believable enough scenario until I recognized one of the names.

Ruth Summerdale. I'd harvested her soul back in the early twenties. She had five, maybe six years left on her contract. That was nothing. There was no way she'd jump ship. Not this close to retirement and on the verge of a celebrity rebirth.

My brow furrowed as I read the rest of the article. Souls being nabbed from both sides of the grave, and no one knowing how or why had everyone in a panic. No wonder they were staying out of sight.

"Here we are, girl." Skipper parked the car in front of Reapers Inc. and turned back to face me. "That'll be eight big ones."

I gave him a coin with ten marks left on it and told him to keep the change. Then I stepped out onto the vacant sidewalk with Saul close on my heels.

The damage Reapers Inc. had suffered in the zombie soul stampede last fall was still under repair. Scaffolding hung from the skyscraper in several places, and a few of the windows with more serious cracks had been taped off, awaiting replacements.

I pushed through the front doors, wanting to get the meeting over and done with as quickly as possible. It was probably delusional to think that Bub and I could make it back to the houseboat in time for dinner, but a quiet night at home didn't sound half bad.

Saul found a corner in the downstairs lobby and circled it a few times, giving it a good sniff before lying down. He rested his muzzle across his paws and yawned. It was our new routine whenever I had to stop at the office. He wasn't fond of the elevators, and Jenni threw an even bigger fit than Grim had whenever I brought the hounds to work with me—especially after Coreen's helljack puppies chewed a leg off one of our dining room chairs. Something about all the antique furniture at Reapers Inc. amped up Jenni's canine prejudice.

I took an elevator up to the seventy-third floor, the Afterlife Council Headquarters, and Maalik met me as I stepped into the fancy hallway that led to the meeting rooms. His gray wings bunched up behind his shoulders. I'd seen them do that enough to know that he was unpleasantly surprised by my presence.

"You shouldn't be here," he said in a hushed voice, taking my arm and steering me into a less visible corner of the foyer.

"Ow. Do you mind?" I jerked my arm free and glared at him.

"Why do you always seem to show up at the worst possible times?" Maalik pinched the bridge of his nose and sighed. His dark hair was unruly, and his robe was spotted with coffee, but at least he didn't smell. Adjusting to the life of a councilman was a gritty process—especially for an upstanding sort like him.

"I was summoned by *President* Fang," I said, rolling my eyes. "So, if you've got a problem with me being here, take it up with her."

I made to leave, but he grabbed my arm again. "You don't understand. You can't go back there right now."

"You're such a drama queen. I'm *supposed* to be here right now. A nephilim guard interrupted my vacation to insist I get over here. I'm sorry if that's a problem for you."

Maalik looked pained, but he let me go this time, choosing instead to follow me down the hall to the main conference room. Muffled voices slipped through the door. They didn't sound overly happy, but I entered anyway, refusing to back down now that I'd had to argue my way this far.

The enormous meeting table was crowded with familiar faces. Cindy Morningstar and Holly Spirit both glanced up and gave me forced smiles. Parvati's smile was more genuine, but she was pleasant to everyone. The Green Man and Kwan Yin were at the table too, but they were too focused on Ridwan, Maalik's fellow Islamic angel, to notice my arrival.

"Rules are rules," Ridwan shouted, before turning his twisted face in my direction. His surprise quickly shifted to malice. "What is *she* doing here?"

"I requested her presence," Jenni said from the head of the table. She rubbed a hand over her forehead and squeezed her eyes shut. "You can wait in my office, Lana. We're almost done here."

"The hell we are!" Ridwan's wings flapped crossly, and he stabbed a finger in my direction. "Her very existence is a breach of the peace treaty and needs to be dealt with. Immediately."

My breath caught in my throat as everyone's eyes zeroed in on me. I'd dreaded this day ever since Khadija had revealed the illicit nature of my purpose. The truth was out, and the poker faces staring back at me weren't comforting in the least.

CHAPTER THREE

"Politicians and diapers have one thing in common.
They should both be changed regularly,
and for the same reason."
—José Maria de Eça de Queiroz

I was less resistant with Maalik as he led me away from the conference room and up to Jenni's office on the seventy-fifth floor. The sound of my heartbeat pulsed in my ears, and I was only vaguely aware of Maalik as he filled me in on the finer details of the council meeting.

"Horus is not in attendance because his station is being challenged, as well. Ridwan is petitioning the council to unseat him and mark him as a traitor, due to his underhanded dealings with Grim—and you." Maalik gave me a sideways glance as we stepped into the elevator.

I leaned against the glass wall and sighed. "Do they really count as *dealings* if I was being blackmailed? He threatened to out me to the council."

Maalik scowled. "Why didn't you tell me? I could have helped."

"How?" I held out my hands. "By being even more overbearing than you already were? Besides, Horus wasn't wrong about Khadija's replacement. Winston was unstable on the throne. He wasn't a true, original believer, and Grim was in no hurry to replace him. Something had to be done."

"Horus should have brought the matter to the council." Maalik's wings fluttered as his back straightened. "Instead, he let the promise of souls—souls he had no right to—buy his silence. He brought this on himself."

"I suppose you think I deserve what's coming to me, too?"

Maalik's shoulders slumped, and he looked away from me. Before he could say anything, the elevator doors slid open, exposing us to the lobby of Reapers Inc. and a brooding glare from Ellen over the top of her desk.

My friendship with Ellen had been strained since Grim's disappearance. She hadn't particularly seemed to like our former boss any more than I had, but Jenni wasn't much of an improvement in Ellen's book. The new protocols and filing system were driving everyone nuts, but Ellen definitely got the worst of it. I guess the evil you know really is preferable sometimes. She clearly blamed me for the changeover.

"I don't have a docket for you today," Ellen said, glancing down at her schedule book. "You're marked down for vacation—and if that's changed, I wasn't informed. It's not on me."

I shook my head. "I'm not here to collect a docket. Jenni called me in for a meeting."

"You and half the city." Ellen harrumphed and fingered a smudge of ash on her blouse. Duster, her pet toy phoenix, had resurrected recently, but there wasn't a pet groomer in the city willing to handle the temperamental bird.

Maalik opened Jenni's office door for me, and a hoarse sob trickled out to greet us. Inside, Meng Po was hunched over in one of the guest chairs with a box of tissues in her lap. Naledi sat on the edge of the other chair making soft, soothing sounds as she rubbed a hand over Meng's back.

"Where's Jai Ling?" My heart went off like an alarm, pounding in my ears again.

Meng's sobs intensified as Naledi gave me a scathing look. Maalik closed the door behind us and put his hand on the small of my back, encouraging me to gather in closer. The room felt too warm, and the heat seemed to come from Meng's grief, radiating outward. I'd never seen her so distraught.

"Gone," she gasped in between sobs. "Taken."

Naledi patted her arm. "Shh, now. Lana will get her back. Won't you?" she asked, turning her dark eyes up at me again.

"Wha—?"

"Absolutely," Maalik said, cutting me off. "I'm sure that's why Jenni summoned her here. There's nothing to worry about," he added, giving me a strained smile and squeezing my elbow pleadingly.

"Right," I said through clenched teeth. "But first, I need to know a few things." *Like why the hell all the odd jobs keep getting forked onto my overflowing plate.*

Meng sniffled and blinked a few times, clearing the tears from her eyes. "She good girl, my Jai Ling. She go to market to buy fish and not come back. Last night, before dinner."

I glanced up at Naledi. "Okay. Maybe you should take her home to rest for now."

"Take the *back* way," Maalik said, raising his eyebrows. "The council is out and about, and they're in a delicate flux at the moment. Meng needn't worry over their turmoil right now."

Naledi winced. "The council frowns on my ability to manipulate the travel restrictions. Jenni has asked that I refrain."

"The council has also refused to fully accept her as their president or you as their peer," Maalik said. "So, expecting you to follow their orders through her seems a bit hypocritical, don't you think?"

Naledi tilted her head to one side. "Good point."

She stood and helped Meng to her feet. Maalik and I both offered a hand to assist, and where the stubborn old gal would have normally berated us for our courtesy, she made a point to thank us all, profusely.

"I know you will find her," she said, hiccupping mid-sob. "I know she okay."

I swallowed my doubt and tried to give her a reassuring smile. Naledi dug a coin out of her pocket, and a few seconds later, she and Meng vanished from the room, traveling through the channels that only the soul on the Throne of Eternity could access.

"Tell me you have more to go on than that," I said, turning back to Maalik. "And remind me again why this is my responsibility."

The angel managed a look that was both apologetic and scolding. He deposited himself on one of the abandoned chairs with a frustrated huff, his wings flapping open suddenly and then settling again. "Meng Po trusts you. Assigning you to the task of finding her lost soul was the only way to keep her from having an outright meltdown." His eyes rolled up to meet mine again. "Also, I need more leverage if I'm to protect you from the council. You must show them how invaluable you are."

I snorted. "You want me to win their favor through good deeds? What do you call everything I've done over the past two years?"

"It's not enough." Maalik pressed his palms together as if in prayer and then lifted his hands to tap his forefingers on his chin. "I'm sorry."

I swallowed the lump forming in the back of my throat and sat down beside him. "So, you really think finding Jai Ling will keep the council from executing me?"

His brow furrowed, and he wet his lips. "It's not just Jai Ling. If you want to prove yourself to the council, you need to uncover the soul-trafficking ring responsible for *all* of the recent disappearances."

"Shit." I rubbed a hand over my face and leaned back in the chair. "This is Ridwan's doing, isn't it?"

Maalik nodded. "I'm afraid so."

"It had to be him. The one member I was sure you'd have the most influence over."

"I'm not a puppet master, Lana."

Angry tears tickled the corners of my eyes, but I blinked them away and cleared my throat. "Well, lay it all out. I need to know who's gunning hardest for me."

"Cindy Morningstar is still burned that you exposed her undercover mission with *Beelzebub*." He winced at having said my lover's name aloud. "And Holly Spirit's opinion of you has not been overly favorable since your close encounter at Holly House."

I'd almost forgotten.

Last fall had been chaos. The rebels hadn't been fooled by Bub's undercover ruse for long, and they'd used him to demand ransom from me in the form of the throne soul.

My attempt to rescue Bub had made me one of Limbo City's most wanted for a short time, and it had resulted in a dicey run-in with Holly at my condo when she unlocked the front door for the Nephilim Guard to search the place. I eluded them before too much damage was done—and I just *barely* grazed Holly with my axe.

My name was cleared soon after, and though she didn't have me evicted, Holly was certainly less warm and bubbly when our paths crossed now. She wasn't thrilled about Bub shacking up with me either. His manor in Tartarus had been destroyed by rioters, and his flat in Pandemonium had been rented out to another demon. Where was he supposed to go? It wasn't like he actually *enjoyed* living at Holly House, where he had to walk past an eight-foot fountain spouting holy water every day.

Maalik frowned as he continued down the list. "Kwan Yin has a formulaic voting method that is troublesome. She often votes in opposition of Meng Po as if to cancel out their collective voice for the Zen Senate and remain neutral."

"Like the fucking Switzerland of Eternity. Super."

Maalik grinned dryly. "The Green Man's voting method is similar, in opposition of Horus."

"What? Why?"

"The Summerland Society has been advocating for some time now to unite with the Sphinx Congress and merge their territories. They hope to persuade the Egyptians to move forward by way of their aggressive voting methods." Maalik shook his head. "I sincerely hate politics. I should have stayed in Jahannam."

My cheeks warmed at the silent accusation. I knew I had been a deciding factor in his initial move to Limbo City, and even though it had been beyond my control, I felt guilty for the outcome.

"Well." I slapped my hands on my knees. "That makes five out of nine—out of eight if Horus gets the shaft. Guess I'm fucked."

Maalik's brows knit together, and he placed a hand on my shoulder. "I think Morgan, the young Summerland soul in Naledi's circle, might be able to change the Green Man's vote. And finding these missing souls would most certainly appeal to Kwan Yin's merciful nature. It might even sway Holly Spirit."

"Right."

"Don't lose faith." Maalik gave me a tender smile, but it was cut short as Jenni entered the room.

Her hair was coming loose from her chopsticks, and the circles under her eyes looked even darker than they had when I first arrived that morning, the bags heavier.

"Your brother is becoming a serious pain in my ass," she said, shooting a dirty look Maalik's way. "First, I'm not worthy of the presidency, then Horus isn't worthy of his seat on the council, and now Lana isn't worthy of the breath in her lungs. What exactly is his angle?" She dropped a stack of files on her desk and sank into her chair.

Maalik shook his head. "He came here expecting transparency and honesty."

"Boy is he in the wrong profession." Jenni smirked and leafed through her paperwork without looking up at me. "I take it Maalik's filled you in on why you're here?"

I shrugged. "More or less."

"Good. I'm reassigning Asha Dipika to the Posy Unit so you and Kevin can focus entirely on uncovering the soul-trafficking ring. I expect you to select a new captain to take your place by tomorrow morning—"

"A new captain?" My head snapped around in time to see Maalik's pained expression.

"Our chat hadn't progressed that far yet," he said sheepishly.

"You mean you didn't want to be the one to break the news." I turned back to Jenni. "Why am I being demoted, exactly?"

"It's not a demotion." She sighed and finally looked up at me. "You're going to be captain of a new unit—Special Ops. You'll work closely with the Nephilim Guard, and you'll have Kevin at your disposal, as well. If and when the council allows for more reapers to be introduced, I'll assign you another charge. Until then, you'll have to make do."

"Wow. This is a lot to digest." I pressed my lips together. "I don't even know where to begin with the missing souls."

Jenni leaned over and reached under her desk. She came back up with a box crammed full of files, placing it on her desk with a grunt. "Here are copies of all the reports taken by the Nephilim Guard over the past three months. I suggest you wrangle Kevin and start going through them. The council expects you to deliver a plan of action Monday morning."

"Is that all?" I asked, unable to keep the tension out of my voice.

"No." Jenni folded her hands over the paper wasteland on her desk. "I also need you to visit Naledi's throne realm tomorrow morning so she can revoke your ability to see a soul's significance."

I sucked in a startled breath. "Can she do that?"

"She's going to try."

"Would that stop the council from executing me?"

Jenni sighed. "Ridwan will likely still push for a vote, but it could improve your odds."

I really hated Ridwan. For an angel, he was a total asshat, and it didn't help that most of his hatred toward me stemmed from my previous romantic involvement with Maalik. I couldn't tell what bothered him more—that Maalik had dated me in the first place, or that I had immediately moved on to a demon after our breakup. Either way, he was hell-bent on seeing me suffer.

Maalik's hand found my shoulder again. "We're doing everything we can, Lana."

CHAPTER FOUR

"If I had my life to live over again, I'd be a plumber."
—*Albert Einstein*

The walk home was surreal. Saul was quiet at my side, sensing my unease. An overwhelming combination of fear and excitement worked my nerves into a nauseating jumble, and the barren streets provided little distraction from my thoughts.

Could Naledi really take away my unique powers? She had enough original believers within reach to secure the Throne of Eternity, so I wasn't exactly needed in that department anymore. Plus, being an ordinary reaper would make the council view me as less of a threat. But did I really want to be an ordinary reaper? For the longest time, I sure thought so. Now, not so much.

A work demotion was one thing, but a voluntary demotion in physical ability just seemed wrong. Like agreeing to have a hand cut off.

The nagging little voice that used to constantly remind me of the gaping caste gap between Bub and me had made an unwelcome return, as well. Would he still feel the same way about me if I gave up the gift that set me apart from the crowd of cookie-cutter reapers engineered for the harvesting trade? Would *I* feel the same way?

The something extra Khadija had bestowed on me changed the way I viewed the world and my place in it. I had purpose and drive—after decades of ambivalent depression. What would become of me if I lost that spark? Could I function as well without it? Would I even *want* to?

I dragged my feet on the way to the condo. Living at Holly House didn't seem so glamorous now, knowing that Holly was planning to vote me out of existence. At this point, I wasn't sure if ending my lease would be a good idea or a bad one. Bub hadn't exactly invited me to live with him at the new manor in Tartarus, but he had asked for my input during the design phase, on everything from the window dressings to the stones used for the walkway. Maybe I could stay there for a while, at least until I found another place in the city. Besides, he'd been living with me for months now. It was only fair, right?

The thought lightened my grim mood, and by the time I made it to Holly House, I was feeling a little better about life—despite the looming possibility of my demise, and the scheduled loss of my special soul vision. I stepped inside the condo and nearly jumped out of my skin.

"He's out!" Gabriel was perched on the back of a sofa in the living room. His wings flapped as he pointed a blue foam finger at the television and howled like a wolf. A handful of Cheetos hit him square in the face.

"Stuff it, messenger boy," Kevin shouted from the opposite couch.

Ross, the captain of the Nephilim Guard and Gabriel's roommate, chuckled softly at their banter, while the helljack puppies snuffled through the shag rug to snatch up the fallen Cheetos. The television was so loud, none of them had heard me come in. Ambrosia Ale bottles overflowed out of the trash can and lined the breakfast bar counter, and a trail of popcorn stretched from the kitchen into the living room.

I waited for the cheering crowd to fade to commercial before dropping the box of files down on the kitchen table. Everyone jumped, and Gabriel fell off the back of the couch, barely flapping his wings in time to keep from busting his ass on the hardwood floor.

"You're home early," Kevin squeaked. "I was going to clean up after the game."

"It'll have to wait. I need your help." I patted the box of files and grimaced.

"Is this about the missing souls?" Gabriel asked, nudging away the helljack puppies as they tried to lick stray popcorn kernels off the hem of his pants. "Holly mentioned something about a new unit, but she didn't say you'd be heading it up. That's quite a promotion."

"Not if she votes to have me executed first." I slumped down at the table.

"Do what?" Gabriel's feathers ruffled, and his cheeks flared pink. "Where are you getting this nonsense? Holly would do no such thing."

I gave him a tired glare. "A trusted source on the council."

"Horus," he growled.

"Maalik."

That set him back a step. "I'll speak with her."

"Thanks." I ran my fingers over the spines of the files in the box. "In the meantime, I guess I should get started on this, you know, just in case I don't get the axe."

Ross lifted an eyebrow at my workload. "Would you like me to send up a guard or two to help? Jenni did mention something about a collaborative effort with the new unit."

"That would be great." I gave him a weak smile before nodding to Kevin. "Why don't you start up a pot of coffee?"

"Sure thing, boss." Kevin didn't sound overly enthused, but he waited to lodge his complaints until after Gabriel and Ross had left.

"I know this isn't what you had in mind when we talked about eventually changing fields," I said as I unloaded the files and stacked them into piles on the table.

"And I was so close to joining the million souls club." He pulled several mugs down from the cabinet with a dejected sigh. "Do you think we'll be doing any harvesting at all with this new unit?"

I shrugged. "Maybe. I really don't know much about it yet, but I imagine Jenni will give us some freelance work between special assignments."

"I sure hope so." He fixed up two mugs of coffee and then joined me at the table. "So, what is all this?" he asked, sliding a cup toward me.

"Missing soul reports and CNHs. There have been more of both lately."

It wasn't entirely unexpected. The dispersed rebels needed a new objective and some quick coin. Snatching souls and selling them on the ghost market was an obvious move, but the volume of high profiles was concerning. It alluded to something more organized than a few rogue demons, especially if they were this good at staying off the radar.

I thumbed through the files, skimming them for familiar names before discarding them on the table.

"What are you looking for?" Kevin picked up one of the files and opened it, glancing over the photo and the scribbled report inside.

"Right now, Jai Ling," I answered, digging out another handful of files.

Kevin looked skeptical. "Meng Po's servant girl? Do you think she would have run off?"

I shook my head. "Meng can be abrasive, but she cared about Jai Ling, and Jai Ling cared about her. The last time I spoke with her, she was really excited about all the things she was learning." My eyes froze on the other name I was after, and I paused to flip open the file.

"Did you find her?" Kevin asked, leaning over to have a look.

"No. I harvested this one almost a hundred years ago."

"Six years out from retirement. Bummer." Kevin shook his head. A knock came at the door, and he jumped up to answer it.

"Ross sent me." Abe's reluctant voice drew my attention away from Ruth's file.

He filled the doorway, even with his stunted wings tucked in against his back. I almost didn't recognize him in his civilian clothes. The shiny body armor the Nephilim Guard wore made them look like majestic creatures. I had no idea Abe was so solid beneath it. I also had no idea he was a redhead. The guards' crested helmets revealed little more than their eyes and jawline.

"Seems an odd choice," I said, frowning as he circled the table. "Why you?"

Abe stuffed his hands in his pockets. "Probably because no one else wanted to work with you."

"You mean you're it?"

Kevin snorted. "Probably because no one else wanted to work with *him*."

Abe gave him a dirty look, but he didn't refute the claim. It was likely true—and my fault. I'd bet he had even been suspended for a while after I escaped his security detail last fall. The fact that it hadn't crossed my mind until now made me feel like a jerk.

I pushed a chair out with my foot and nodded at the mess of files. "Welcome aboard."

Abe's eyes narrowed, and he shook his head as if surprised, but he sat down. "What would you like me to do?"

I pressed my fingertips against my temples and tried to invoke Jenni's logic. "First, we're going to sort through these and pull all the factory soul files. We'll keep Jai Ling in the mix since she disappeared from the city, too. Then I want to organize them chronologically."

"What good will that do?" Kevin asked.

"I'm hoping a pattern will appear. Or maybe the files will slide together like one giant jigsaw puzzle, revealing the name of the culprit. I don't know." I rolled my shoulders and stretched my neck from side to side.

Kevin shrugged and cleared a spot at the opposite end of the table. He set the empty box there, and we used it to filter out the files on souls nabbed from the mortal realm or the afterlives. There were at least twice as many of those, which was why I wanted to tackle them last.

Abe didn't say much, but he turned out to be competent with clerical work. I wondered what kind of job he had before joining the Guard. I couldn't picture him as a pencil pusher, though he did express a fondness for our tasty dark roast brew—twice—which led me to believe he'd been overexposed to the crappy break room variety found in the cubical industry.

After an hour of quiet shuffling, we were left with forty files that spanned the three months in question. That seemed like a lot—which I guess is why we were asked to look into it in the first place.

Abe stood and stretched his wings with a yawn, while Kevin fired up another pot of coffee. I stayed at the table, grimacing at the rows of neat files and scratching my head.

The numbers hadn't revealed much yet. Eight souls had been taken in January, nine in February, and then twenty-three in March. Someone had gotten greedy and drawn too much attention in the process. I doubted Jenni would be impressed with that revelation. There had to be something more I wasn't seeing yet.

"You want another cup, boss?" Kevin asked, glancing over his shoulder as he refilled his mug.

I shook my head. "Four is my limit. I'll have to start naming my ulcers if I drink more than that."

Abe's wings fluttered. "I'll take one more."

Kevin brought the carafe to the table and then handed it over to Abe when the doorbell rang. The churchy tune curled Abe's lips down distastefully, but his expression changed when Kevin opened the door for Warren, the nephilim who crafted the Guard's weaponry and swanky gear for me on occasion, as well.

"Afternoon, all," Warren said, looking just as surprised as Abe. He gave his feathered brethren a polite nod before focusing his attention on me. "The repairs on your bike are finished. Also, I was wondering if you'd mind testing a prototype in the field for me." He held up a wooden box and gave me an anxious smile.

Warren had gifted me the bike, presumably as a thank you for setting him up at Holly House where his talents were soon discovered, and he rose to stardom. I should have known it would cost me down the road. He'd asked me to try out everything from restraint charms to retractable cloaks. I'd learned enough in my time as a guinea pig to know he should have stuck with weapons.

Warren was a genius, but even geniuses struck out on occasion…or in some cases, a lot. I really loved the bike, but I wasn't sure how much longer I could handle being the crash test dummy for every little idea that popped into Warren's head.

I turned away from his expectant face and scratched my arm. "You know, I'd love to, but I just got transferred to a new unit. Our first assignment is pretty sensitive, so it may have to wait a bit."

"I understand." He set the box down on the only bit of kitchen table not covered in files. "Just take a look whenever it's convenient. I think you'll like this one."

I gave him a tight smile and nodded. "Thanks for stopping by. We better get back to work."

Abe finished off his cup of coffee and cleared his throat. "Actually, I have to take off. Harbor gate duty tonight. But I can help more tomorrow," he added with a questioning look.

"I have an appointment in the morning, but I'll give you a call after if we need you," I said, my stomach churning as I remembered my upcoming procedure with Naledi.

Warren opened his arm to Abe and stepped back into the hallway. "I'm heading downstairs to the gym. I'll walk you out."

Abe nodded at the mess on the table as he left. "Good luck with that."

Kevin closed the door after him and gave me a peculiar look. "You're a little green. What's going on in the morning?"

"Nothing you need to worry about." I turned away from him and snatched up the wooden box Warren had left behind. It was slightly larger than a shoebox and easy enough to wedge in with all the scarves and hats crammed on the top shelf of the coat closet. When I turned around, Kevin was still watching me. "What?" I snapped.

He pressed his lips together and frowned. "Is this appointment before or after you announce the new captain of the Posy Unit?"

Great. I still had that to deal with.

"After," I said, deciding I probably wouldn't be up for anything other than sulking once Naledi purged me of my superpowers.

Kevin picked the coffee pot up from the table and returned it to the burner. "Do you know who you're going to choose yet?" he asked.

"Arden."

Without a doubt, he was the one for the job. It occurred to me that I should probably call him and let him know so he'd have time to prepare, though he had been filling in while I was on vacation, so he already had the docket prep work down. He'd probably want to meet up early to go over a few additional things. I wondered if I'd have to give up my office space. And just when I'd finally gotten the place decorated the way I liked. It figured.

Kevin made a pained face and opened the refrigerator to put away the creamer. "Kate's going to have a fit."

I shrugged. "Dealing with Kate's attitude will be Arden's problem from now on. His Zen master demeanor should put a real crick in her neck."

Picturing the two of them having it out—or rather, Arden ignoring Kate's juvenile antics—made me smile. Kate and I'd had a rocky start. We were by no means besties now, but we'd eventually settled into a comfortable, mutual disinterest. Hey, it worked for us. It probably wouldn't so much tomorrow morning, but that couldn't be helped. Arden was the reaper for the job, and truth be told, he should have had the position all along.

Keys jingled at the front door, and my mood perked. I hadn't seen Jenni at the condo in weeks, but Kevin had given Bub Josie's key last month. My apprentice still struggled with his grief from time to time, but he was making progress. Turning over Josie's key had been a milestone, considering that he was still hoarding all of her clothes in our storage unit.

Bub entered the kitchen with a devilish grin on his face and a cheery hum in his throat. "Miss me, love?"

"You have no idea." I linked my arms around his neck and gave him a kiss. Kevin was still in the kitchen, so I kept my tongue in my mouth, not wanting to encourage the gagging noises he seemed to make every time Bub and I showed affection.

"What do we have here?" Bub asked, tilting his chin at the files on the table.

"You don't want to know. Hell, I don't want to know." I groaned and pulled away from him, putting my hands on my hips as I turned to glare down at the files.

Bub let out a long sigh. "Guess we won't be picking up where we left off, after all."

"Nope."

Coreen trotted around the corner and peeked in on the helljack puppies snoozing on the living room rug before coming to find me. She ran her wet nose under my hand and yawned, casting a lazy glance at the food dishes beside the refrigerator. Saul had been eyeballing them for a while now, too.

I tried to be quiet as I scooped some Cerberus Chow out of the bag in the coat closet, but the helljack puppies were on me before I'd made it halfway across the room, licking at my ankles and whimpering.

"Good grief, Kevin. Didn't you feed them today?" I asked, trying not to spill the kibble as I tripped over my own feet.

"Do Cheetos count?" Kevin gave me a guilty grin and ran a hand through his mop of hair. I was glad he'd grown it back out, but his boy-band charm still didn't work on me. I glared at him as I filled the hounds' dishes.

"They're sleeping in your room tonight. Maybe you'll think better of it after their horrific gas wakes *you* up in the middle of the night."

"Agreed." Bub snorted as he watched the pack of hounds dig in, shoving each other aside greedily. Food scattered across the hardwood floor, and the puppies left the bowl long enough to chase each morsel down.

Kevin shrugged and went back to the refrigerator, opening the door to rummage about. "Cheetos are the only thing I've been able to train them with. They hate those charred hellcat bones you get from Hades' Hound House. They smell like burnt tuna casserole."

Bub pointed his cane at him. "That's not as bad as the smell that's going to wake you up later."

"Whatever." Kevin found half a sandwich hidden in the cheese drawer. "I'll be in my room if you need me," he said, taking a hearty bite as he left the kitchen and headed down the hall.

Bub wrapped an arm around my waist, pulling me in closer now that we were alone. "We could always stay the night on your ship," he whispered.

I looked down at the files on the table again. "I really can't. Maybe Monday night, hopefully after I'm done with this mess."

Bub pouted, pushing his bottom lip out. "Fine. I'll let you get back to it, but I do expect you to take a break to have dinner with me later."

"I don't know how much time I'll have to spare. I need to look over all this again, and I have a few calls to make."

"We can order in." He gave me a vexed look.

"Okay. I suppose I can carve out twenty minutes," I said.

Bub rolled his eyes. "So much for our vacation."

My thoughts exactly.

CHAPTER FIVE

I spent the rest of Saturday evening looking over the soul files, then rearranging them and looking over them again. And again. I sorted them by the time of day the souls had gone missing, by the day of the week, and by the day of the month. I was sure a pattern would emerge.

I took a five-minute break to inhale a meager helping of the Thai food Bub had ordered, and then spent another five minutes on the phone with Arden, letting him know that he was the unit's new captain. He didn't break into a fancy acceptance speech or anything, which would have been entirely out of character for Arden, but I had expected a little more excitement than I was met with.

"You're sure there's no one better-suited? Molly is quite experienced, and she's two centuries older than I am," he said after an awkward pause.

"You've been with the unit longer, and everyone respects you. Are you refusing the job?" I snapped. Another long pause followed.

Finally, he said, "No. I accept."

We hung up shortly after. Arden didn't do small talk, and I had my hands full with the inane file shuffling. By the time I called it quits, a migraine had set in, and Bub had already fallen asleep.

Coreen stayed with her pups in Kevin's room, but Saul was stretched out across the foot of my bed, Bub's bum leg propped up on Saul's belly, rising and falling in time with the hound's breath. I snuggled in with them, letting their warmth comfort my aching mind.

I wasn't sure why, but I felt guilty for not saying anything to Bub about Naledi's plans for me in the morning. I tried to convince myself that I was being ridiculous. That nothing would change. That the paranoid cartoon playing in my head, where I left the condo in Technicolor and returned in black and white, was a gross exaggeration.

After all, Bub hadn't known I was any different from other reapers until I told him as much. It wasn't like Naledi was removing my nose. There was no way Bub would be able to tell just by looking at me that I'd lost my soulish x-ray vision. I'd work up the nerve to tell him down the road when my complex over the whole ordeal had faded.

I woke up the next morning before Kevin or Bub and made coffee and cinnamon rolls, pretending it was because I was such a nice boss and girlfriend, and not because I felt guilty for keeping secrets again. Then I took a quick shower and left early for the harbor to meet with Arden before the rest of the unit showed up.

The sky was still shrugging off night, and light dew clung to everything, enhancing the earthy smell of spring. Clusters of daffodils and tulips bloomed out of barrel planters lining the sidewalk outside Holly House. A soft breeze whipped through the courtyard, causing the cherub fountain full of holy water to mist my cheek.

Warren shouted good morning to me from the entrance of the parking garage as I headed for the travel booth across the street. I waved back and adjusted my messenger bag on my shoulder as I widened my steps, hoping to avoid a pop quiz on the mystery gadget I hadn't looked at yet.

I took the travel booth to the one near the harbor entrance and exited out onto Market Street just as the streetlights flickered off, letting the daylight take over. The scent of the sea mingled with freshly baked donuts, no doubt coming from Nessa's shop up the way. My stomach grumbled, and I found myself wishing I'd swiped a cinnamon roll before leaving the condo.

An unfamiliar nephilim stood at attention near the harbor entrance, and I wondered when Abe's shift had ended. Nightshift guard duty had to be the most boring thing ever, and for his sake, I hoped Ross would assign him to the new unit permanently.

There weren't many reapers lingering on the dock this early. Most did freelance harvesting and coined off as soon as they reached the harbor. The other three specialty units had their own routines. Santos Consuelo, the captain of the Lost Souls Unit, bought his crew coffee at the Phantom Café every morning. Guess we all knew who'd be getting the boss of the century award.

I made my way down the main pier of the dock and found Arden waiting for me on the deck of my ship. His skin was as black as the robe he wore, creating an ominous silhouette against the thin morning light bleeding up the horizon.

"Congratulations on your promotion, Captain Harvey," he said, offering me his hand as I came on board.

"Congratulations on *your* promotion, Captain Faraji," I replied, giving his hand a firm shake. "Are you excited to be working with Asha again?"

Arden had previously worked with Asha Dipika, his sailing partner, on the Mother Goose Unit, exclusively harvesting child souls. I got the feeling Arden missed it. As reserved as he could be, whenever a child soul ended up on the Posy Unit list, he would speak up long enough to volunteer for the harvest.

"Asha is not happy about the transition," Arden said, his forehead crinkling. "She has relented for the moment, but I suspect she will be petitioning President Fang soon. As it stands, she's scheduled to begin with our unit tomorrow."

I nodded. "I hope she knows this wasn't my doing. None of it was." I leaned against the deck railing and crossed my ankles. "There's not much I feel I can share with you that you don't already know better than I do, but if you have questions, ask away."

Arden opened his mouth hesitantly. If his skin weren't so dark, I would have sworn he was blushing. "Does President Fang know you selected me as the new captain?"

I raised an eyebrow. "Not yet, but I planned to tell her this morning."

He nodded slowly. "When do the captains converge for their weekly meetings?"

"We meet with Jenni individually. I check in on Tuesday mornings, so my best guess is that she'll brief you then."

"Tuesday?" Arden said tightly.

"Yup."

There was clearly some gossip to be had there, but the reaper was as tight-lipped as they came. Plus, the rest of the gang decided to arrive about then. I'd have to harass Jenni later until she divulged.

Kate Evans and Alex Grayson headed up the band of merry reapers. They'd been on the Posy Unit the longest. When Adrianna Bates, the former captain, had left to take over the Mother Goose Unit, Kate had been sure that the vacancy was hers. She was a fifth-generation reaper, but her childish demeanor seemed to cause everyone to forget that fact.

Molly Driver and Tyler Ives were the newest additions to the team and the only reapers who had been on the unit for a shorter time than I had. My placement as the unit's captain had been controversial for a number of reasons, the least of which being that new captains were typically chosen for their experience within a unit. Yeah, I didn't have any. It definitely didn't endear me to anyone.

Horus, the Egyptian god on the council, had pulled some strings—though not because we were such good buddies. It was all part of his elaborate blackmail scheme. Now that that plan had been put to rest, there was no reason for me to stay. Still, I was a little bummed to be taking a step down.

Special Ops was too new to be taken seriously yet. We hadn't even completed our first mission. And if we couldn't, there was a good chance the unit wouldn't survive long enough to even warrant a shitty article in *Limbo's Laundry*.

Kevin strolled up the ramp behind the others. He didn't have the hounds with him, which seemed to tip everyone off more than anything else.

Alex glanced around the deck and rubbed her hands up her arms to stave off the morning chill. Her eyes narrowed when they fell on me. "What are you doing back so soon?"

"Passing the torch," I said, nodding to Arden. "Meet your new captain."

Arden gave me a hard look as if he'd expected me to break them in more gently. Sleep deprivation seemed to shorten my patience and drain what little tact I possessed.

"Can't be any worse than you," Kate said, folding her arms. She tossed her bangs back and gave me a daring sneer as if anticipating a comeback.

I shrugged. "You're probably right. Well, have fun. Come on, Kevin."

"That's it?" Molly's mouth dropped open. "That's all you have to say to us? No explanation? No departing well-wishes?"

I paused and let out a long sigh. "I've been ordered to head up a new unit. Arden is an exceptional reaper, and he'll make a great boss. He's wise and fair and even-tempered. I sincerely do wish you all well. Even you, Kate," I added, glancing back at the brooding reaper. "I have an appointment to keep, and you have souls to harvest. If you want a bigger to-do, catch up with me at Purgatory later, and I'll buy you a drink." I gave them a little salute and took off before anyone else could object.

Kevin skipped beside me to keep up. "Where're we going, boss?"

"You're going back to the condo and taking another look at those files," I said, heading for the travel booth outside the harbor entrance. "I have an appointment."

Kevin raked a hand through his hair. "So you keep saying. You sure you don't want me to come with?"

"No." I stepped inside the travel booth and turned around to face him. "I'll check in when I can. And I'm serious about looking over those files," I said, jabbing a finger in the air.

I waited for Kevin to stalk off down the sidewalk before fishing my ID card out of my bag. The secret throne realm wasn't so secret anymore, and the council had insisted on adding it as a destination in the booths. Of course, it required special clearance, so the ID cards had been implemented.

The council, or more specifically, Ridwan, had made a stink when Naledi requested a card for me. She reminded him that it was her realm to do with as she pleased, and that she could, in fact, do whatever she pleased with all of Eternity if he wanted to push the issue. That changed his tune, but it also added another black mark next to my name in his book.

I inserted my ID card into the slot on the travel booth dashboard and then dropped a coin into a wider slot. It cost nearly three times as much to travel to the throne realm versus just venturing across the city. That was probably breaking Ridwan's bank more so than my own, though, so I didn't mind.

The travel booth spit me into a newer, recently installed one on the edge of the sunny lawn in the throne realm. It was strange not to immediately and haphazardly find myself in the grass. I peered through the streaky booth glass and took in all the new construction.

The size of the realm hadn't changed much, but with all the souls Naledi had been collecting for her Apparition Agency, the accommodations had needed an update. The little cottage that had housed Khadija for over a thousand years—and then Winston for a short span—was still there, but three additional structures had been built into the surrounding knolls. They looked fit for hobbits, and I was sure Morgan was right at home, seeing as how many of the fey were hill dwellers.

Naledi waved to me from the front porch of the cottage as I stepped out of the booth. She was in a pair of navy slacks and a white, button-up blouse—clearly pieces from the new wardrobe Jenni had helped her put together. The vagrant hand-me-downs she was prone to choosing for herself were not inspiring much respect from the council. The new look was definitely more polished, and it added an air of maturity that she hadn't possessed before.

"Everyone's waiting inside," she said.

"Everyone?"

Naledi nodded. "Jenni, Maalik, Ridwan—they all insisted on being present. I told them it wasn't necessary." Her brows drew together. "I can make them leave if you want."

"It's okay." I swallowed and walked up the stairs to the porch. Naledi squeezed my arm, and we headed inside together.

I hadn't spent much time exploring the cottage. When Khadija had lived there, the fear and awe she filled me with had instilled too much respect for me to poke around. Winston, on the other hand, had been such a little shit that I couldn't wait to leave.

My heart hurt when I thought of him and the way he'd given up his life in his search for Naledi after she had disappeared last fall. She'd explained her reasons, and they were sound enough, but it still made me twitchy around her sometimes.

"This way," she said, leading me past the foyer and the great room.

The dark hallway near the back of the cottage was new territory for me, and I was surprised to find a circular stairwell at the end of the passage. It led down into darkness, and I half expected Naledi to fetch a lit torch. When she flipped a light switch, I stifled a laugh.

Naledi grinned. "I made them update the electrical in here when they put in the new abodes."

We followed the stairs down to what I felt comfortable calling a basement rather than a dungeon now, with its modern upgrades. The floor was polished stone, but fresh paint covered the walls, and the door Naledi opened at the bottom was new and didn't creak.

We entered a large room that featured what looked like a massage table. Jenni and Ridwan were arguing in a corner.

"How are we supposed to know if this procedure even works?" the angel said, waving a hand at the table.

Jenni's jaw flexed. "We'll bring in some souls and test her if that will make you feel better."

"She could lie, and we'd never know." He turned to watch me come into the room and snorted his displeasure. "She's been hiding it from us for this long. What's to stop her from doing so again?"

"Are you doubting my abilities?" Naledi asked, stopping beside me. She folded her arms over her chest and glared at Ridwan. He glared right back.

"I'm doubting your intentions," he said.

"We're not here to fight." Maalik put himself between them and held up his hands. "You asked to observe," he said to Ridwan. "So, observe."

Ridwan pressed his lips together and lifted his chin, turning away from us. His wings shuddered violently like a disgruntled rooster.

Naledi directed me over to the table. "You'll be more comfortable if you lie down."

"Is this going to hurt?" I asked, dread swirling in my stomach. I'd been so worried about the aftermath that I hadn't even considered what the process would be like.

Naledi gave me an apologetic smile. "It's not going to tickle, but I'll do my best to make it quick. I can also wipe your memory after so you don't remember the pain."

"Why didn't you ask Meng to whip up a tea for that?" I asked, handing her my messenger bag for safekeeping.

The table didn't look so inviting now. I frowned as I eased back onto it and folded my arms over my stomach.

Maalik stepped in closer and took my hand. "There was some concern that it might affect the results." His eyes flicked up in Ridwan's direction. "But I'll be at your side the whole time, for moral support."

"Thanks," I said, trying not to let my voice crack. I didn't like showing weakness, least of all in front of Maalik, but I had no idea what I was in for. Even I wasn't foolish enough to presume that everything would be okay.

Naledi rubbed her hands together and then held them palms down over my torso. "Ready?" she asked, giving me a tender look.

I swallowed hard and nodded. My eyes rolled up to the ceiling, trying to find a source of distraction. It worked for a few seconds. The wide plane of drywall was lit by an inset light that ran around the perimeter of the room, almost like a fancy home theater. I tried to picture Naledi, Morgan, and Father Ron having a movie night down here and grinned.

Then the sound of static filled my ears, and my body tensed like it was trying to solidify into concrete. I felt Maalik's hand squeeze mine as a high-pitched noise tore through my head. It wasn't until Maalik shouted my name that I realized the sound was coming from me.

CHAPTER SIX

*"Alcohol is the anesthesia by which
we endure the operation of life."*
—*George Bernard Shaw*

I awakened upstairs in the great room of the cottage. There was a soft ringing in my ears, and everything was too bright, like when you wake up from a nap at the beach and the sun's peeking past the rim of your umbrella.

"Hey there." Morgan sat on the couch opposite me, her legs folded up beside her as she read from an old book, the leather cover split and peeling away in places. In her vintage, red dress, she looked like a gothic Alice in Wonderland.

"How long have I been out?" I asked, sitting up and rubbing the sleep from my eyes.

"About two hours," Morgan said, glancing back down at her book. "You just missed Maalik. He left ten minutes ago."

"Where's Naledi?"

"Meeting with Horus. I'm not supposed to know, but *I hear things*," she finished in a sing-song voice. "She said you're supposed to take it easy and rest up for the meeting tomorrow morning."

There was a general tenderness throughout my body as if maybe I'd fallen down a flight of stairs. My joints felt numb and loose, but there were no obvious bruises anywhere. A fading pins-and-needles sensation itched along my skin, and I tasted sweat on my lips.

As my eyes adjusted, I took a closer look at Morgan, really focusing on her outline where her aura should have appeared. Nothing.

"Super." I found my bag on the coffee table and pushed myself up from the sofa. As I stumbled for the door, I added a headache and dizziness to my list of side effects.

My last memory was of Maalik's worried face looming over me. I guessed Naledi had gone ahead and removed the rest of the ordeal. It was probably for the best.

I walked across the lawn in a daze and took the travel booth to Holly House. Part of me wanted to lie back down and take another nap, but the more responsible part wanted to see if Kevin had discovered anything new from the files.

Warren appeared in the entrance of the parking garage again as if he'd been waiting there for me since I left that morning.

"Heya, lady!" he called. "You check out that soul gauntlet yet?"

"The what?" I lifted an eyebrow as I punched in my code on the security box.

"The prototype I dropped off yesterday," he said, opening the front door for me.

"I told you, I'm in the middle of a big assignment. I haven't even been in the field since we last spoke," I said, quickening my pace toward the elevators as much as my dizziness would allow.

"Okay, well, let me know when you get a chance."

"You bet." I fingered the up button and impatiently watched the floor numbers descend.

Warren headed back to the garage with slumped shoulders, passing Holly Spirit along the way. Her eyes twinkled with ill intent, and she managed to slip inside my elevator before the doors could close me in.

"You're looking well," she said, her lips curling up with false cheer. Her wings fluttered delicately and folded against her back, right under the mound of golden curls pinned at the base of her neck. "How did your procedure go?"

I frowned and inched away from her. "Okay, I guess."

"Ah, that's right. Ridwan said your memory was altered. That must be terribly disorienting." Her angelic eyes took on a mocking softness.

"I'll be fine. At least I don't have to worry about the council viewing me as a peace treaty breach anymore."

"Now you just have to face judgment for conspiring with Grim."

I tried to hide my loathing behind a smile, but my face pinched uncomfortably. "Another accusation of Ridwan's, I'm sure. Guess I'm lucky there are eight other members on the council besides him."

"Seven." Her smile grew sharper. "Horus has been suspended until his own trial."

The thinly veiled allegation made me bubble with anger. I wasn't a big fan of Horus. Hell, I had more reasons to dislike him than most. But Holly rubbing it in that I was short an ally made me want to press all the buttons in the elevator so she'd have a nice long journey back to the lobby.

The doors chimed as they opened onto the tenth floor. I stepped out into the hall, eager to get away from Holly and her plastic persona.

"Feel better soon," she called after me as I hurried toward my condo.

I nodded, not trusting my voice, and stuffed a shaky hand down into my bag to find my keys. As soon as I heard the elevator doors close, I paused and leaned against the wall of the hallway, waiting for the dizziness to pass and my heart to slow its murderous march.

I was so done with Holly House. If I survived the council's decision, I was out of here. But I'd let Saul take a steaming shit on the white rug in the living room first. Pet deposit be damned.

I entered the kitchen, grumbling my evil plans under my breath, and found Kevin slouched in a chair at the dining room table. The files, which I'd left in neat rows, were now a disaster. Most of them lay open, their guts spread out and scattered to the point that there was no way to tell which folder they belonged to.

"I got nothin', boss," Kevin said, dragging his hands down his face until his eyes sagged miserably. "I was at the very top of my class. I really thought I'd find something and save the day."

I shrugged. "Me too, grasshopper. Maybe we just need a palate cleanser."

"Huh?" He cocked his head at me.

"Go grab your jacket."

Kevin didn't argue. He headed back to his room while I filled the hounds' dishes with kibble. I didn't expect to be back in time for dinner.

I hurried Kevin downstairs and through the lobby, not wanting to risk another encounter with Holly or Warren. Feathered company just wasn't rubbing me right today. Maybe having my status reduced, however secret it had been, made me resentful. I wasn't a special snowflake anymore, and I needed time to let that fact sink in.

The sidewalks outside were still light on soul traffic. How strange that a lack of ghosts made it seem more like a ghost town than ever. It was the sort of philosophical question I would have enjoyed discussing with Josie. My throat tightened as I cast Kevin a sideways glance, wondering if he thought of her as often as I did.

The quiet of the inner city allowed the sounds of the sea to reach us, and we enjoyed the music of the waves and the distant clattering of bills as several storks returned to the Three Fates Factory.

Purgatory Lounge was empty, but at least it was open. Xaphen, the demon who ran the place, waved at us from his usual post behind the bar.

"Be with you in a minute," he shouted as he finished drying a glass and placed it on a shelf along the mirrored back wall.

Kevin and I picked a booth near the front. We didn't go out and drink much, especially not since his hellfire problem had been brought to my attention. He'd been clean for six months though, so I tried not to beat myself up too much for having him tag along. No one likes to drink alone.

"What'll it be, kids?" Xaphen asked, setting a basket of peanuts on the table between us.

"Pitcher of Ambrosia Ale and four shots of demon piss," I said and then glanced at Kevin. "You hungry? I'm buying."

"Wanna share a basket of wings?" he asked.

I nodded and turned back to Xaphen. "And a basket of wings."

The old demon nodded and headed for the kitchen, while Kevin twiddled his fingers together on top of the table. He snatched a peanut and set to work prying open the shell.

"I really shouldn't be drinking hard liquor," he said, his eyes lowering nervously.

"The shots are for me. It's been a rough day."

"The mystery appointment?"

I thought of Ridwan and Holly. "Among other things."

The jukebox clicked over as if out of boredom and began crooning out an oldie, while the traffic outside the front window increased. It was quitting time for most reapers, and they slowly began to filter through the city upon returning from their harvests.

Just as Xaphen delivered our drinks and wings, the bell above the door jingled. Kate poked her head around the corner and spied us at our table. Alex was a step behind her. She looked embarrassed to be standing outside on the sidewalk with passing reapers gawking at her.

Kate tossed her bangs back and raised an eyebrow at me. "Does that drink offer still stand?"

I contained my smirk and looked up at Xaphen. "Could you bring us another pair of mugs?"

Kate and Alex stepped inside, and Kevin moved around to my side of the table so the two of them could sit together across from us. After Kate's rude comment that morning, I had to wonder if she'd just dropped by to see if she could gather gossip fodder about the new unit.

I nudged a couple of the shots across the table toward them and then lifted my own. The limey green liquid had a fizz to it, and it tickled my fingers as we clinked glasses.

"If I should stumble out this bar, I pray the night is worth the scar," I said, tossing the drink back. Kevin pushed the remaining shot my way, and I drank it, too. I could tell it was going to be one of those nights.

Alex made a sour face as she sat her empty glass down hard on the table. She shook her head, wiping the sleeve of her robe across her mouth, while Kate squinted as if trying not to cringe. Her competitive nature never seemed to stall, but if she was looking to challenge me tonight, she was going to pay for it in the morning.

"I got the next round," Kate said, waving her hand in the air to catch Xaphen's attention.

The front door jingled again, and the wind caught it, throwing it wide open. Chatter drifted in off the sidewalk, bringing another lot of familiar faces with it. Molly, Tyler, Arden, and Asha made their way to our booth. Their baggy, black robes blended together, forming a dark curtain that dissected the room and blotted out the light from the front window.

"Look at that!" I said, a bittersweet tinge taking hold in my chest. "The whole gang turned out. Drinks all around."

"We can't stay." Arden glanced back at Asha. Her face was a stony mask, and her arms were folded. Arden placed a hand on her shoulder and looked back at me. "I just wanted to congratulate you again and thank you for your service on the Posy Unit. It has been an honor working with you."

"Same to you." I shook his hand and tried not to notice how Asha refused to make eye contact with me. Somehow, I'd known I would catch the blame for her transfer.

Arden and Asha left, but Molly and Tyler stuck around a bit longer. I hollered for Xaphen to bring another pitcher and more glasses, and we all scrunched together in the booth. Molly sat beside me, while Tyler crammed in next to Kate.

"So, you're captaining a new unit?" Molly asked after ordering a bottled light beer from Xaphen. She gave the sticky bar table a questionable look and folded her hands in her lap.

"Special Ops." I tossed back another shot and nodded, shivering as the booze hit the back of my throat in an explosion of tart lime and sugary sweet watermelon.

Kevin gave me a wary look as if he were concerned I might overshare. I wasn't that drunk. Yet. But there really wasn't much to share, so I wasn't worried about where my mouth might wander off to later in the night.

"I figured we were just a rung up on your ladder to the top," Kate said. Alex gave her a scolding glare as she matched my shot.

The comment didn't bother me. Everything Kate said was scathing to some degree, so I'd stopped taking it personally a long time ago. I grinned back at her and downed another shot, knowing Alex would drag her out of the bar long before I was ready to call it a night.

Tyler reached for the pitcher of ale and filled a mug. "Not many reapers to spare in the field these days. Who else did they recruit for the new unit?"

"The Nephilim Guard." I paused to hiccup. "And maybe a reaper baby, if the council approves another lot to make up for our losses."

Kevin made a face at my baby comment, but it was true. He hadn't been a reaper two years yet, which meant his apprenticeship would last another ninety-eight. That thought alone had me reaching for another drink. As expected, Kate followed suit.

"Here's to those who wish us well," she said, holding her shot glass out to knock with mine again.

"All the rest can go to Hell," I finished with her.

Xaphen dropped by the table and swapped out our empty glasses with a tray of fresh ones, including a dozen more shots and another basket of wings. Kevin had almost polished off the first batch. I imagined it was in an attempt to distract himself from all the liquor. I pushed the fresh wings his way, too.

Tyler helped himself to one of the green shots and raised it high, waiting for us to join him. Kevin and Molly passed, but Alex reluctantly picked one up after Kate and I did.

"You can deal with the devil," he began, inspiring more than one eye roll around the table. Everyone joined in, reciting the most cliché of reaper toasts. "Or pray with your last breath. But time will catch you soon enough, there is no cheating death."

We threw our shots back, and senseless laughter followed, as was standard whenever booze flowed freely. Molly's smile grew tense as she finished off her beer. She shook her head when Xaphen tried to bring her another.

"I have dinner plans tonight, and I'd like to change first," she said, standing up from the table.

Kevin's eyes anxiously followed her, his one sober companion at the table. "I should take off, too," he said, bumping my arm to encourage me to stand so he could crawl out of the booth. "I'd like to go over those files one more time."

It was a lame excuse, but I didn't give him a hard time. Kate, Alex, and Tyler were company enough for now, and I felt less guilty about pushing shots on them.

I patted Kevin on the back as he stood up from the table. "If you happen to see Bub at the condo, tell him where I am, and that he's welcome to join me," I said, sliding back across the pew.

Tyler came around to my side to give Kate and Alex some breathing room, and we all waved as Kevin and Molly left. A handful of nephilim slipped past them, laughing as they approached the bar. One was in a guard uniform, and he lifted his nose in the air when he spotted me.

As someone who had previously shrugged their detail, I wasn't popular among the Guard. Not even after my name had been cleared. Guess that didn't make much difference when it came to showing them up. I considered buying the whole bar a round to break the tension, but then decided that buying Kate's booze was penance enough.

She lifted another shot glass and cleared her throat. "Don't know if I've lied to the angels. Don't know if I've lived in sin. But when the devil comes a-knockin', Lana's just gotta let him in." She tossed the drink back, and then coughed as she tried to giggle and swallow at the same time.

I snorted and drank my shot, immediately grabbing another once I'd finished. "May you eat when you're hungry, drink when you're dry, find a coin when you're hard up, and grow a soul before you die."

Kate paled as she tried to keep up with me, the green liquid leaking past the corners of her mouth. Alex gave me a disapproving glare and pushed the tray of shots back from their side of the table.

"I haven't had a good bender in a while, but I can certainly say I've not tied one on this quickly before," Tyler said, holding a shot glass in each hand. He wasn't as desperate to show his ass as Kate was, or rather, he didn't realize he was on the sidelines of a pissing match.

"I'm hungry," Alex said, reaching for one of the menus tucked behind the dusty condiments bin. "What would you like, Kate?"

"A fuzzy navel." She giggled and poked Alex in the ribs. "Maybe your fuzzy navel."

Alex pushed her hand away and blushed. "I meant to eat."

"Hmmm." Kate's eyebrows wiggled, turning Alex an even deeper shade of red.

"Kate," she said in a warning voice.

"You're right. That's for dessert."

Alex tucked her face down in the menu and grumbled, but her words were cut off as the jukebox fired up again, pumping out a classic rock ballad.

"I love this one," Tyler slurred as he beat his fingers on the table like drumsticks. "You know, I was in a band for a few decades during my apprenticeship."

"You don't say?" I grinned and sipped at my beer, trying to ignore the fact that it took entirely too much effort to get the glass to line up with my mouth.

Tyler nodded. "We were good, too. Ghostman and the Grims. All-reaper ensemble, except for our front guy, Ghostman," he said, wobbling on the pew as he leaned closer to me. "He was a factory soul, obviously."

"Ovi-obi-*obviously*." I snorted out a giggle, and we clinked glasses.

Alex poked her head over the menu she was studying. "I think I might have one of your albums. *Dead but not Forgotten*?"

"That'd be us!" Tyler pumped his fist in the air. "I was the bass player. We broke up after Ghostman's contract with the factory ended. I hear he made it big on the other side. Went on to be a pop diva or something."

"He was reborn as a girl?" Kate snickered. "Bet he loved that."

"Yeah." Tyler scratched his head. "Guess the contract only stipulates what family you're born to. The rest is up to the Fates."

Xaphen brought a fresh pitcher of ale and took Alex's food order. I could tell he was thankful for the business, but he didn't seem thrilled about the third tray of shots I ordered, though he brought them, and we continued our drunken conversing.

More nephilim and reapers wandered in as the evening grew late. A few minor deities made an appearance too, but no souls, reminding me that I was responsible for finding out who was snatching them up. It put a kink in my good mood that I tried to smooth out with more booze.

The front door jingled fiercely, and Bub suddenly appeared at the end of our table. His dark slacks and satiny dress shirt were too swanky for Purgatory, but fortunately, he'd skipped the suit jacket. He gave Tyler an appraising glare and then lifted an eyebrow. "I believe you're in my seat."

"Oh!" Tyler stumbled out of the booth and tripped over the hem of his robe as he squeezed in with Kate and Alex.

Bub hooked his cane on the edge of the table and sat beside me. Confusion crept over his face as he gave me a once-over, but it soon shifted to amusement. "Are you…drunk, my love?"

"What? No," I lied, rolling my eyes. They were practically floating.

Xaphen returned with a basket of fried okra and onion rings for Kate. "Good to see ya, Bub. What are we havin' tonight?"

Bub rested his arms on the table and tapped his fingertips together. "An Old Fashioned would be lovely."

Xaphen hurried off, leaving the table in silence. My colleagues didn't know how to act around the Lord of the Flies.

They traded anxious frowns, and I had to think fast to stave off the awkwardness.

"Give us your best toast. We've run out," I said, handing out green shots from the tray in the center of the table.

"You've run out?" Bub grinned. "So you *are* drunk."

"Whatever. I'll drink you under this table." I held a glass out to him, trying and failing not to sway.

"Hmmm." Bub took the shot and raised it. "May you never go to Hell, but always be on your way."

"I'll drink to that," Kate said.

We touched glasses over the table, and the sticky green booze sloshed over the rim of my glass and trickled down my hand and wrist. I drank the shot, spilling more of it in a line across my cheek.

"Oh, dear." Bub sighed. "You're going to be a handful tonight, aren't you?"

I groaned and laid my head on his shoulder. "It's been one hell of a day, and I just want to forget the whole thing."

"You seem to be well on your way," he whispered and pushed a curl away from my face, tucking it behind my ear. "But Kevin tells me you have a meeting with the council in the morning."

"Kevin's got a big mouth," I said, pushing myself upright again. "Where's Xaphen? We need more shots."

Xaphen returned with Bub's Old Fashioned. The flames along the demon's brow danced nervously as our eyes met.

"Would you be an angel and bring us another tray of demon piss, Xaph?" I hiccupped and tried to bat my eyelashes, but the gesture felt too complicated for my stupefied state. I probably looked like I had something in my eye.

Xaphen raised an eyebrow at Bub in question. It disappeared beneath his crown of flames.

"What are you looking at him for? He's not paying for them, I am," I said, trying for an indignant tone that came off more desperate than anything else.

Bub pressed his lips together and sighed. He gave Xaphen a short nod. "One more tray, then I'll get her home."

"One?" I whined. "No one ever lets me have any fun."

A sharp wind hit my face, and then Gabriel was in the bar, his wings folding up neatly against his back. He was in a crisp robe, not his usual drawstring pants, and I couldn't spot a single wrinkle—or Cheeto stain for that matter. His brooding eyes took in our table with blatant disapproval.

"What are you doing here?" I slurred. "Thought the Board of Heavenly Hosts didn't want you consorting with the riffraff 'round these parts."

"I can go wherever I choose to," he said, his chin held high. "I just refrain from making a fool of myself in public. You should, too."

I swirled my finger in the air mockingly. "Whoop dee doo. Reputations are highly overrated. I should know."

Gabriel stepped forward, the judgey look in his face shifting to worry. "Lana—"

"Drink with me," I said, holding out a shot glass. "If you can do as you choose, like you say, share one of your famous toasts with us."

Gabriel's jaw flexed, and his nostrils flared, but he took the glass and touched it to mine. "To absent friends." He drank his shot slowly, watching me over the rim of his glass.

A lump found its way into the back of my throat, and even the shot couldn't make it go away. In fact, it seemed to make matters worse. Gabriel knew my weaknesses, and he wasn't afraid to exploit them if he thought it was for my own good.

"That's it?" Tyler frowned at the sullen angel. "You've been known as the Angel of Ale for, like…the past century. That's the best toast you've got?"

"The Angel of Ale?" I put a hand over my mouth, but I couldn't muffle my laughter. "How have I not heard that before?"

"Because most know better than to say it within earshot," Bub said, watching as Gabriel's expression grew wrathful.

CHAPTER SEVEN

*"I don't like to commit myself about heaven and hell—you see,
I have friends in both places."*
—Mark Twain

Gabriel's eyes glowed with holy rage. A year ago, being called the Angel of Ale wouldn't have bothered him at all. Hell, he probably would have answered to it. But now that he was aspiring to holier things, the insult clearly stung.

"Uh-oh." I giggled, too drunk to keep my mouth shut at this point.

Alex shoved her leftover onion rings in front of Tyler and stuffed one into his mouth, cramming the entire thing past his lips. "Don't mind him. He won't even remember this conversation in the morning," she said, giving Gabriel a strained smile.

Tyler mumbled a protest around the onion ring, but whether it was at her statement or the force-feeding was anyone's guess. Kate shook with silent laughter, and Alex elbowed her in the ribs hard enough to earn a grunt and a belch.

"I think I might be sick," I said, leaning my head against Bub's shoulder again.

Bub pushed his half-finished drink away. He dropped a heavy coin next to it and then stood, pulling me along with him. The pew was slippery, and I had trouble slowing the trajectory of my ass along its polished surface. Bub wobbled on his feet a moment before reaching for his cane.

"Let me help," Gabriel snapped. He still hadn't warmed to my demon lover, but exchanging words of any sort with him was a vast improvement.

Bub looped one of my arms over his shoulders and wrapped a hand around my waist, leaving his other free to hold his cane. He nodded at Gabriel. "If you'd like to take her other side—"

Gabriel grumbled under his breath as he hooked my right arm around his neck. They dragged me toward the front door, but I dug in my heels, skidding them across the floor.

"I need to say goodbye, and I haven't paid yet." I twisted around, straining to see the booth.

"I left enough coin for us both," Bub said through clenched teeth. His brow furrowed as he hobbled backward, turning our little trio in a wide arc to face the booth. Alex, Kate, and Tyler watched us with peculiar expressions. I shouldn't be surprised. A demon and an angel escorting a loaded reaper out of a bar wasn't something you saw every day.

"Reap on!" I shouted to them, taking my arm away from Gabriel long enough to throw my fist into the air. Tyler returned the motion, unable to speak due to the onion ring he was still choking down.

Kate lifted one of the green shots at me, waving it with a teasing sneer. "Happy harvests!"

"Good luck with the new unit," Alex added, putting a hand on Kate's arms to lower the dripping shot glass out of her face.

"Thanks, scythe sister!" I said over my shoulder as Bub turned us toward the door once again. Xaphen tossed us a casual salute from his spot behind the bar as we stepped out onto the sidewalk.

Above the clustered buildings, the sky was a dusty gray, as if a storm were trying to roll in. Zibel, the local weather god who worked at Bank of Eternity, ordered up rain this time of year for the city park. The precip usually came in the middle of the night, so as not to inconvenience the citizens of Limbo City. Ah, the perks of living in a prefab afterlife. Intelligent design at its finest.

Bub struggled to keep up with Gabriel's long gait down the sidewalk. He didn't rely on the cane as much as he had at first, but he still wasn't one hundred percent. Having me sagging on his shoulder probably didn't help matters.

"I can take her," Gabriel said, his voice loaded with venom.

"I know how to walk." I shoved away from them both and stumbled a few steps ahead, my hands held out to keep my balance. I swatted Gabriel away as he swooped in to assist.

We walked to the end of the block, and Bub caught my arm as I tried to step off the curb and cross Morte Avenue. "Travel booth is this way, love."

"Home is that way," I said, pointing in the opposite direction.

"Quite right, but the closest travel booth is up near the park." He pointed his cane north, toward the sidewalk that curled around the corner and led up to Council Street.

I let him turn me around, and we began walking again. Bub stayed at my side, while Gabriel remained a few steps behind, his hands shoved down into the pockets of his robe, and a deep scowl creasing his face.

When we reached Holly House, Gabriel punched in his security code to get us into the building. I staggered as we waited, my balance somehow worse now that we were no longer in motion. The garden lights blurred my vision, and I blinked several times to clear my eyes.

"I can't believe Holly hasn't evicted me yet," I said out loud, mostly to myself.

Bub took my hand and folded it over his arm. "You're a good tenant. You pay on time. You don't make a lot of noise. She has no reason to evict you."

I shook my head, stopping short when the world began to spin. "Is hating my guts not a good enough reason?"

"Holly doesn't hate you," Gabriel said as we entered the building. Charlie, the nephilim who managed the place for Holly, glanced up from his desk and gave us an odd look. He waved slowly, mostly to Gabriel, and watched as we loaded into an elevator.

"Holly *totally* hates me," I said once the doors had closed. "She told me so today."

"She did?" Gabriel's eyebrows scrunched together, and his feathers ruffled skeptically.

"Well, not in those exact words, but she made it pretty clear. That's why I'm gonna give her my thirty days' notice tomorrow."

"What?" Bub's head whipped around, and he pressed a hand to the mirrored wall to steady himself.

Gabriel snorted. "So much for your freeloading."

Bub ignored him, and a soft grin took over his face. "Does this mean you're moving into the Tartarus manor with me?"

"She'll do no such thing," Gabriel snapped, his wings ruffling again.

"Yup!" I threw my arms around Bub's neck and gave him a wet kiss. He returned it with gusto.

"Ick." Gabriel covered his eyes with one hand and turned away. "Can't you two wait until you're out of my line of sight?"

"Gonna be one *hell* of a housewarming party," I said, twisting around in Bub's embrace to slug Gabriel on the arm. "You better be there, too."

"Whatever. You're not moving to Tartarus. Jenni will flip out."

"She's not the boss of me—well, not all the time." The elevator doors chimed as they slid open onto the tenth floor, and I did a cartwheel down the hallway, nearly taking out a lamp on a side table.

Gabriel hurried after me to run interference, putting himself between me and the next table. "If you don't keep it down, Holly *will* evict you," he whispered harshly.

"What do I care? Home is where the hellfire burns!"

Gabriel looked like he was ready to murder me. He ground his teeth together and cast a nervous look at Bub. "Speaking of hellfire, guess who I ran into this afternoon?"

"Your demon girlfriend?" I shot him a nasty warning look, but he didn't waver.

"Maalik." He paused to see how Bub would react before going on. "He told me about what happened this morning."

My stomach did a little flip, but I wasn't sure if it was anxiety or the booze not agreeing with my acrobatics. "That wasn't his place," I said, digging for my keys as we reached the front door to the condo.

"What happened this morning?" Bub asked, the giddy humor now gone.

"Nothing you need to worry about." I hated how defensive I sounded, but I wasn't ready to talk about it yet.

I entered the condo with Bub and Gabriel in close pursuit. It was dark inside, save for the light above the kitchen sink illuminating a pile of dirty dishes. Kevin was probably already in bed. The hounds, too.

I braced myself against the back of a dining room chair and kicked off my boots. The files that had been spread out over the table were tucked back inside their box, and I was reminded of my meeting in the morning—yet another disaster that had inspired my binge-drinking.

"You should have told me, Lana." Gabriel closed the front door behind us and turned around, folding his arms over his chest. "I should have been there with you."

Bub looked from Gabriel to me. "Would someone kindly explain what I missed?"

I opened my mouth, but I couldn't get anything to come out. I hadn't planned on telling him like this. Not now. And certainly not drunk.

Gabriel exhaled a long sigh as if considering how much I'd already shared with the Lord of the Flies. "I take it you know about Lana's…true purpose?"

Bub's eyebrows shot up. "The Throne Soul is common knowledge now, and while I doubt Lana's affliction is as well-known, it's hardly a secret. At least not among the council and subcommittees."

Gabriel's chin lifted, but his eyes went soft. "Affliction? Well, you can consider her cured, then."

I slumped onto a barstool at the kitchen counter and buried my face in my hands.

"What do you mean?" Bub demanded. The sound of his boots on the hardwood was loud as he crossed the room and stopped beside me. "What is he talking about? And what does it have to do with the Keeper of Hellfire?" He looked back to Gabriel for answers.

Gabriel squeezed my shoulder, but I shrugged him off and rubbed my fingers under my eyes, wiping away angry tears.

"Why can't you mind your own business?" I sniffled and ran my hands through my hair. I couldn't bring myself to look at either of them.

"I'm sorry," Gabriel said. "I'm not trying to start a fight. I just want to understand why you didn't tell me—or *him*, for that matter," he added, grumbling in Bub's direction.

"And why does Maalik know?" Bub pressed, his voice slipping dangerously close to a whine.

"Because he's on the council," Gabriel said in a tone that suggested he wanted to add "*duh*" to the end.

Bub glared at him a moment before his eyes filled with worry, and he turned back to me. "Are you okay?" His hand found my shoulder, but I didn't have the heart to shrug him away like I had Gabriel.

"I'm fine. It's fine. Okay. No big deal. Just one less reason for the council to bother with me, right?" I tried to laugh, but the sound stuck in my throat.

"Maalik said it looked painful." Gabriel decided to take his chances and grasped my opposite shoulder again.

All the touchy-feely was making me claustrophobic. I gasped in a ragged breath and cleared my throat. "I don't re-member. Naledi wiped my memory of the procedure."

"Small mercy," Bub said, stroking his fingers down the back of my arm. "Would you like me to run you a bath? Fix some soup or tea?"

Gabriel rolled his eyes and huffed. "She's not sick, stu-pid."

"That would be nice," I said to Bub, running my hand under my nose to wipe away the tears and snot accumulating there. He kissed my forehead and headed off for our room, looking relieved to be away from Gabriel.

"Do you have to be such a jerk?" I asked Gabriel once we were alone.

"I can't help it." He gave me an apologetic look and sat on the barstool next to me. His wings arched and then settled against his back again, resting on either side of the stool. "I didn't like him before he went undercover with the rebels, and I find I don't like him any better now that he's back on our side."

"Can't you try? Please?" I sniffled again and pierced him with my watery gaze. "I'm serious about moving to Tartarus. Bub and I have been through a lot together, and despite everything, we're doing great. I love him—"

"Don't say that." Gabriel groaned and looked away from me with a scowl.

"I love him," I repeated. "And I love you, too. But he's trying to be civil, and you're not. You're an angel, for Pete's sake—"

"Do you have to bring him into this?" Gabriel's lips pinched together—in mock anger this time.

"Really?" I said, trying not to smile at his joke.

"Okay." Gabriel sighed and folded his hands over the counter. "I'll try. Happy?"

"Very." I hugged myself and managed a weak smile.

A splattering sound drew our attention to the window in the living room. The storm had arrived. It began as a gentle sprinkle but quickly grew into a downpour, streaming across the glass in thick rivers.

Gabriel's arm folded around my back, pulling me in for a hug. "I still wish I had been there for you. Even if you don't remember it."

"I didn't know how to tell you—or anyone." I rested my chin on his shoulder and closed my eyes.

The rain filled the silence that fell between us. Soon, Bub returned to let me know that my bath was ready. I said goodnight to Gabriel, staring him down until he reluctantly shook Bub's hand in farewell.

"That was a first," Bub said under his breath as we passed Kevin's bedroom door and headed through our room to the attached bathroom.

"Cherub steps," I said. Bub chuckled and helped me pull my shirt over my head since I wasn't quite sober enough to accomplish it on my own.

After a bath and a bowl of tomato soup, we snuggled up in bed, tucking our feet under the mountain of hounds on the far end. Bub had dressed me in a pair of cotton shorts and a tank top, and he'd stripped down to his boxers. Our limbs tangled together under the sheets, his bare skin warming mine. A giddy lightness filled my chest, and my defenses completely dissolved. So, naturally, that was when he began his interrogation.

"Why didn't you tell me?" he whispered. His eyes glowed softly in the dark, his gaze taking me in with curious concern. "Were you afraid to?"

I swallowed and pushed in closer to him, resting my cheek against his chest. "I didn't want you to think I'm weak."

"Never," he hissed, squeezing his arms around me. "I could never see you as anything less than magnificent."

I swallowed hard and tried to will away the tears threatening my eyes again. "It's just going to take some time, you know, getting used to not being special anymore."

"You'll always be special." Bub laughed. "The council can't take that away from you." He ran his fingers through my damp curls and sighed. "This meeting in the morning, does it have something to do with all those files in the kitchen?"

I crinkled my nose. "I'm supposed to be uncovering the soul-trafficking ring in Limbo City. Jenni thinks it will help my chances with the council ruling—"

"Ruling of what?"

I let out a little gasp, realizing too late what I'd let slip.

"Lana?" Bub said in a low voice, pulling away from me.

I swallowed hard and took a deep breath through my nose. "They're voting whether or not to execute me for conspiring with Grim."

"What?" He jolted upright, but I tugged him back down beside me.

"It's going to be okay," I said, sounding surer than I felt. "That's part of the reason Naledi zapped my powers this morning. And if I solve the mystery of the disappearing souls, I might be able to get enough votes in my favor to keep breathing." A nervous laugh escaped me, and I tightened my arms around Bub's waist.

"I see," he said, his body slowly relaxing again. "Maybe I can help."

"I don't want to worry about it tonight. Just hold me." I twined a leg around one of his and yawned.

Bub nodded, his chin grazing the top of my head. I could sense his worry, but my eyelids were heavy, and I couldn't keep them open any longer. I had a terrible feeling that morning would arrive too soon.

⚔

CHAPTER EIGHT

"Fate is for those too weak to determine their own destiny."
—Kamran Hamid

I loved waking up to the smell of coffee, especially coffee in bed. Bub had enough good sense not to bring me food when I was hungover. He also had the best hangover cure in six hells.

"Drink," he commanded, holding out a glass of what looked suspiciously like orange juice. He held a cup of steaming coffee in his other hand, just out of my reach. "Good girl potion first, then you can have the bean brew."

"*Baaaaarf.*" I made a face at him and fingered back the chaotic nest of curls stabbing me in the eye. That's what I got for going to bed with wet hair. I sat up, pulling my feet out from under Saul's furry butt, and then whimpered as I took the glass from Bub.

The concoction was good at nixing headaches and dry heaving, but getting it down in one gulp was the real trick. The stuff rivaled Meng's first-aid tea, but with a sticky, cough syrup aftertaste that required half a cup of coffee to erase.

I pinched my nose and tossed the drink back, holding my breath as my gag reflex kicked in. "You're evil," I said with a shudder.

"To the core, darling." Bub grinned and presented the coffee to me with a bow and a fancy hand gesture. "But you'll thank me when you get through your meeting this morning without vomiting all over the council."

The meeting. Ugh. I glanced at the alarm clock on my bedside table and cringed. T-minus two hours until I had to face off with the council and share my grand plan for fixing their soul dilemma. The only problem was, I didn't have a plan.

The box of files hadn't revealed anything new that the council didn't already know, and I had a sinking feeling that they were counting on that. The members I hadn't outmaneuvered or intimidated at one point or another were either indifferent when it came to my fate, or they had a legitimate and vested interest in this particular hoop I was trying to jump through. Like Meng Po.

My heart ached a little when I thought of the Lady of Forgetfulness. Even if the rest of the council wanted to see me fail, I knew she was rooting for me. And if saving my neck wasn't enough motivation for her, finding Jai Ling was a worthy cause. I wondered where the soul was and whether or not she was afraid.

Bub shouted to me from the kitchen. "You'll have to get out of bed for your second cup. If you can make it to the coffee pot, I'll know you're awake enough to discuss your plans for today."

"Is not dying a plan?" I threw myself back on the bed and pulled a pillow over my face.

"I think I might be able to expand on that just a bit, love."

It took more effort than I was comfortable with at this hour, but I tossed the pillow aside and threw back the covers. Coreen lifted her muzzle long enough to squint at me through her sleepy eyelids. Then she snorted and curled herself back around the pair of snoring helljack pups. They were more than half her size now, which meant the pack was close to taking over the bed. Kevin would have to step up their training soon, especially if he didn't plan on moving to Tartarus with me. I still needed to go over that little detail with Bub.

I pulled myself out of bed, snagging my empty coffee cup from the bedside table, and shuffled out of the room. When I emerged in the kitchen, Bub was sitting at the dining room table. The files were arranged in several tidy stacks around a yellow legal pad, and Bub hummed as he copied something from a report.

He closed the folder when he finished and grinned up at me. "How much do you know about the factory's incoming delivery schedule?"

My sleep-addled brain was distracted by how Bub's British accent tackled the word *schedule*, and I completely missed his question. "Huh?" I replied intelligently.

His brows lowered into a frustrated line. "Go get your second cuppa, and we'll try this again. Plus, you may want to do something with…um." He waved his hand in a circle over his head.

I glanced up and caught a few of my mangled curls in my peripheral vision. "Oh."

I retreated to the bathroom and found an elastic band to stuff my hair in before returning to the kitchen. "What was the question again?" I asked as I refilled my coffee mug.

"The Three Fates Factory. What do you know about their incoming deliveries?" Bub said, tucking a file back in the box.

I plopped down in the chair beside him and shrugged. "Not much really. I know the afterlives occasionally deliver a few of their older souls for reinsertion."

I thought of the time Asmodeus had intervened and saved me from the clutches of the Fates when they thought I'd stolen Atropos' shears. He had been making a soul delivery, if I remembered correctly. Atropos' grasp on my throat had cut off the oxygen to my brain, so my memory was a little fuzzy.

Bub nodded at my comment. "Yes, some souls tire of their afterlives after so many centuries, and they petition their deities for a chance at reincarnation. A lottery drawing of sorts takes place, and those souls are transferred to the factory. The damned are often returned to the factory too, after they've served their due time."

"Have any of those souls gone missing?" I asked.

"Oh, no." Bub laughed. "Gods rarely allow their most valued residents to depart, so they're in no danger from the poachers. But a soul transfer would make a convenient cover, don't you think?" He pursed his lips.

I took a long drink of coffee and thought on his suggestion. Something about it didn't fit. "That would only allow them to get souls into the city, not out."

"Or—" He raised a finger. "It would allow the culprit to move souls around the city without much scrutiny."

"Why wouldn't an abducted soul resist?" The answer hit me hard between the eyes. "Unless a deity with power over the dead was in on the heist."

Bub lowered his voice. "Or a reaper with soul hypnosis training, perhaps?"

Paul Brom, the captain of the Recovery Unit, also taught the soul hypnosis class at the academy. The skill was a relatively harmless one. Although it made retrieving souls from bodies that had been crushed under debris from natural disasters a little easier, therefore making it a prerequisite for the Recovery Unit.

"I'll check with Grace Adaline and get a list of everyone who's taken the soul hypnosis class. If I cross-reference them with the list of renegade reapers, maybe we'll get a better idea of who we're dealing with," I said.

Bub smiled and pushed the legal pad my way. "This might help, too."

The notes he'd made were divided under headers for various afterlives and the dates of their deliveries to the factory over the past three months. He'd found the pattern. The soul-traffickers were only doing their snatch-and-grabs on days when big deliveries were being made by multiple afterlives. It meant that they also had an intimate knowledge of the factory schedule, and familiarity with the employees, seeing as how they were nabbing the most valuable ones.

"I think I can work with this. Maybe set up some interviews at the very least." I breathed out a heavy sigh, letting the dread I'd been carrying around for the past few days go with it.

Bub gave me a devilish smile and lifted my hand for a kiss. "You're welcome. Now, go get a shower, love. If small children were allowed entry into Limbo, you'd certainly scare them all away with that coiffure. Are you sure you're not part demon?"

"Such a sweet-talker." I rolled my eyes and fingered back a curl that had escaped my ponytail, vaguely wondering if I'd even bothered with conditioner during my drunken bath.

I downed the rest of my coffee and headed for the shower. Kevin's door opened as I passed his room, and he let out a little gasp.

"Morning, boss," he said, struggling to maintain eye contact without laughing.

"Shut up."

"I didn't say anything." He pressed his lips together and shook his head.

I raised an eyebrow at him as I opened my bedroom door, and the hounds came stampeding out into the hall. The sound of kibble echoed from the kitchen, and they took off.

Kevin trailed after them, waving his hand without looking back. "Happy grooming!"

I hurried into the shower, noting the hour I had left to make myself presentable for the council. Hopefully, a bottle of conditioner and a half-baked plan would be enough to get me through the morning.

CHAPTER NINE

"I always arrive late at the office,
but I make up for it by leaving early."
—Charles Lamb

$\mathbf{D}$espite being better prepared, my hands trembled as I punched the elevator button for the seventy-third floor at Reapers Inc. The sudden ascent made my heart stutter, assaulting my equilibrium as if I were on a rollercoaster. It made me wonder if the elevators had always moved this quickly, or if my anxiety was causing me to hallucinate.

I wanted to believe that Jenni would give me a heads-up before the council took their final vote on my fate, but the transition since Grim's spontaneous departure still seemed to be underway, and the new rules hadn't finished their game of musical chairs yet. For all I knew, the council was polishing the guillotine while they awaited my arrival.

The elevator stopped suddenly on the thirty-seventh floor, Grim's former interrogation level. The taste of acid hit the back of my throat as my morning coffee tried to make a run for it. I breathed through my nose, struggling not to hyperventilate as the doors slid open.

Jenni's tired face greeted me. "I've been waiting for you," she said, crooking her finger to urge me out of the elevator. I hesitated, and she gave me a berating look. "I want to talk to you before the meeting. Torture free. Promise."

"Why here?" I asked, crinkling my nose as I stepped out into the faux construction zone. The settling dust was real enough, and it made me sneeze three times in quick succession.

"It's probably the safest place in the entire building to have a private conversation," Jenni said, eyeing the sheets of plastic hanging from the ceiling in place of walls. They were dirty but transparent enough to see if we were truly alone.

I rubbed the goosebumps climbing up my arms and tried not to think about all I'd seen take place on this floor. "What do you want to talk about?"

Jenni stepped over a pile of painting supplies and leaned against the raw edge of the receptionist desk. "The council is really pushing for a verdict soon. This assignment could be the tipping factor for you. Please tell me you have a solid plan."

"I don't know about solid, but I have a plan."

"Well?" she asked, shaking her head impatiently.

"Shouldn't I be telling you at the same time as the council?" I asked slowly. "This doesn't count as conspiring against them or treason, right? I'm a little hazy on the subject after all the finger pointing I've been at the wrong end of."

Jenni clenched her teeth together and rubbed a hand over her forehead. "I'm not asking you to keep the plan from the council. I'm offering to be your sounding board and help you fine-tune it. That's all. Look, if you don't want my help—" She took a step toward the elevator.

"I do! I do," I said, holding my hands up to stop her. "I just want to make sure I'm doing things by the book. I've gotten myself into enough trouble to choke a hellcat, and at least half of that was unintentional."

Jenni sighed and folded her arms, waiting for me to get on with it. I gave her the short version, going over Bub's theory, and the interviews I had in mind.

"Don't mention the Lord of the Flies to the council." Her eyes widened pleadingly, and I stifled a scoff.

"Naledi zapped my soul vision, not my common sense."

"Some might argue whether or not you had any of that to begin with," Jenni said under her breath.

"Hardy har." I gave her a humorless smile. "Anyway, you think that's enough to keep the council off my ass for a while?"

"Ehhh." Jenni shrugged one shoulder. "A couple days at most, I'd say."

"Super."

"Oh, I almost forgot." She held her closed fist out to me, shaking it when I hesitated again. "Morgan asked me to give you this, for good luck."

I opened my hand and Jenni dropped a familiar stone onto my palm. It was the hollowed-out necklace Morgan had given Winston last fall for protection. He'd given it to me in return. With half a twist, the necklace rendered the wearer invisible. Morgan was as worried as I was about the council's intentions.

I swallowed and slipped the necklace over my head, tucking the stone under the collar of my robe. If things went sideways at this meeting, I had a way out now. Maybe Bub and I could steal away to the mortal realm, live out the rest of our days in human territory—at least until council or rebel assassins caught up with us. It didn't sound so bad at this point.

"Come on. Don't want to be late," Jenni said. She glanced down at her watch and pressed the elevator button.

We ventured up in silence. I went over my plan again in my head, while Jenni faced the mirrored walls to fix her hair. There was a lot more I wanted to talk to her about, but now wasn't the time. Maybe after the assignment was finished, if I managed to keep my head.

The doors opened on the seventy-third floor, and we exited into the lavish foyer of the Afterlife Council headquarters. The conference room doors at the end of the main hallway were open wide, and a scramble of divine voices fought for supremacy. The meeting had begun without us.

Jenni took a deep breath and walked toward the room with long strides. Confidence had always been one of her strong suits, but as the new CEO of Reapers Inc., she'd had to amp up her game to stay in league with the council. I trailed behind, attempting to mimic her poise. If I could make it inside the conference room without curling into the fetal position, I'd be content.

The noise became clearer as we approached. Maalik and Ridwan were at the forefront of the squabble, their angelic voices clashing like heavenly cymbals announcing Judgment Day.

"Your needless cruelty is unbecoming, brother," Maalik said. His disapproval always had a patronizing tone to it. I hated it when he used that voice on me, and I could tell Ridwan wasn't a fan either.

"Your bias is not welcome here," Ridwan hissed back. "I have a mind to petition for your vote to be nullified due to your previous relations with the fugitive—"

"The *accused*." Maalik cut him off sharply. "No vote has taken place yet, so *fugitive* is a careless and false label. Who's biased now?"

"Gentlemen," Parvati interrupted. Her silky voice quieted the feuding angels. "We are gathered here today to discuss a more pressing matter."

They all turned to watch Jenni and me enter the room. So many eyes, all filled with different intent. Maalik and Ridwan were the most obvious, having just aired their opinions to everyone. Maalik's expression was equal parts worried and hopeful, while Ridwan emanated pure loathing.

I noticed Horus was still absent from the table, and I wondered if he too planned on jumping ship—or rather, jumping *on* a ship out of here—if his verdict was as unfavorable as I feared mine would be.

Cindy and Holly pasted on fake smiles. Their veiled hostility wasn't fooling anyone, least of all me. Holly was holding a grudge for an accidental slight, and Cindy for a more intentional one—exposing her involvement in Bub's illicit undercover mission.

It was a wonder she hadn't been suspended from the council along with Horus. I had a feeling she was also feeling put out by me stealing Bub away from her cabinet of go-to warriors. Her reluctance to help clear his name had not endeared her to him, and he was currently on a permanent hiatus.

Kwan Yin and the Green Man sat at the far end of the conference table. They both viewed me with neutral expressions. Either they were indifferent about my fate, or they were just that good at hiding their views on the matter. Of course, their views couldn't have been that strong if they were willing to blow their votes to further their other agendas. How comforting to know where my life fell in the grand scheme of things.

At least Parvati met me with a smile. Her presence was openly warm, and she waved her two left hands, welcoming me to take a seat between her and Meng Po, who I was relieved to see had stopped wailing long enough to attend the meeting. Her eyes were bloodshot, and she twisted her aged fingers together over the table as I took the chair beside her.

"What news of my Jai Ling?" she asked, skipping right over the formal introductions and fancy commencement nonsense.

Ridwan looked like he might scold her for her haste, but Parvati spoke first. "Yes, please share what you've discovered."

Jenni circled the room and took the chair near the window, the one usually reserved for Grim. Ridwan made another offended face, but I drew his attention away by clearing my throat.

"Nothing is certain without further investigation, but the reports suggest that someone with extensive factory knowledge is involved, and possibly a deity or a reaper with soul hypnosis training—"

"We went over those files ourselves." Ridwan snorted and leaned back in his seat.

"For weeks," Cindy added, her smile stretching just a little too far. "What makes you think you've found something we missed?"

"This is why I assigned Lana as captain of the new Special Ops Unit. She sees things others don't," Jenni said.

Holly's wings fluttered. "I thought we fixed that little glitch yesterday morning," she said in her sickly-sweet voice. My back went stiff at the taunt. Jenni didn't see the humor in her comment either.

"Naledi removed her ability to view a soul's aura, not her acute perception or her outstanding track record when it comes to solving the council's problems—or have you forgotten?" Jenni looked around the table, making eye contact with each of them. Then she looked back to me. "Continue."

I sat up straighter and tried to remember everything Bub and I had discussed that morning. "The souls are being abducted on busy delivery days at the factory, presumably to use the heavy soul traffic as cover. Since no one has reported seeing a soul being transferred through the city against their will, they are likely under the influence of a death deity or a reaper who has been trained to hypnotize souls. I'd like to conduct several interviews before organizing a sting operation."

"Sting operation?" Meng huffed and gave me a bewildered look. "I want my Jai Ling now."

"We'll find her," I said. "But we also want to bring down the entire ring. If we don't take out the top player, there's a good chance Jai Ling could be taken again."

"I lock her up," Meng snapped. "She never leave temple again. I feed anyone who come for her tea so strong they forget every life they ever know." Her eyes narrowed dangerously, and I knew she would make good on her threat.

"We'll find her," I said again. "We'll find them all. I promise."

"You better," the Green Man said. His voice was deep and smooth, and I realized how little I'd heard him speak before. "My vote for your fate will depend on your results. As I'm sure goes for others on the council."

He glanced around the table, though he didn't seem entirely convinced of his last statement. The green tint of his skin darkened to a brown, bark-like hue, as if he were bothered by the notion that he actually had to make a call of his own now that Horus wasn't available to counter maneuver.

It was mildly reassuring, and I wondered how my verdict would be determined if, by some stroke of dumb luck, I was able to snag the Green Man's vote and get a hung jury. Would they flip a coin? That was less reassuring.

Parvati placed her four hands on the table. "I move that Lana go forward with these interviews and then conduct her operation."

The Green Man nodded. "I second the motion."

Maalik's wings visibly relaxed, and I could tell he was relieved that someone else had taken control of the meeting
besides Ridwan. "All those in favor, say 'aye,'" he said, speed-
ing things along.

Everyone except Ridwan agreed, even Holly and Cindy,
though I imagine they wanted to save face for the moment
and keep their prejudice hidden until a better opportunity
arose to smite me. The near unanimous vote didn't even warrant a call for nays, but Ridwan made up for it by glaring at
me until I was excused from the meeting.

I left Reapers Inc. lightheaded and full of conflicting glee
and dread. I felt as if I'd just cashed in a get-out-of-jail-free
card. Or, more accurately, as if I'd cheated death. It made me
nervous because I knew better than most that death was a sore
loser.

CHAPTER TEN

"I think everyone should go to college and get a degree
and then spend six months as a bartender and six months
as a cabdriver. Then they would really be educated."
—*Al McGuire*

The demon defense course I'd taught at the Reaper Academy last semester was now under the tutelage of Jack, Bub's former butler and Meng Po's current lover—a thought which always made me shudder.

Jack had taken up residence with Lady Meng after Bub had gone undercover with the rebels, and the Tartarus manor was destroyed by rioters. He'd been caught unawares by the whole ordeal. Maalik and I had charged in at the last second to rescue him before the place went up in flames.

Jack had an unusually tender disposition for a demon. We'd left him in Meng's care due to a cracked horn, and the pair had hit it off.

Even after Bub's name had been cleared, Jack still refused to forgive him for departing so suddenly and without notice, and he was most definitely not returning to his previous position as butler for the Lord of the Flies. Not now that he was in love and respectably referred to as Professor Jackson by the students at the academy. The title suited him better than it had me.

The demon defense course took place Monday nights at the academy, so I wasn't surprised when I ran into Jack on my way to speak with Grace Adaline.

"Lana, my dear, it's so good to see you," he said, taking his reading glasses off and propping them up above the two small horns that jutted from his forehead. He gave me a one-armed hug since he was balancing a mountain of books with his other and then smoothed his hand down the lapel of his tweed jacket. "What brings you to the academy? Do you have news about Jai Ling?" he asked in a hushed voice.

"Not yet, but I'm working on it," I said, nodding at Grace Adaline's closed office door. "I have some questions that need to get answered before I can get to the guns-a-blazing part of the plan."

"Very good." Jack glanced around nervously and stepped in closer, tucking his stack of books under his chin. "Poor Meng is just beside herself. I've never seen her so devastated. It breaks my heart. Please, if there's anything I can do to help, just name it." He removed a hand from his books again long enough to squeeze my shoulder.

"Thank you."

I watched him toddle off down the hall toward his classroom, and then I knocked on Grace's door.

"It's open," her muffled voice called from inside.

I cracked the door and poked my head in. For as meticulous as Grace could be, it was alarming to see her office in such disarray. To be fair, finals were drawing near, and the war had created complications for the academy, as well. Several of the reapers who had previously taught classes were now too swamped with overtime harvesting, thanks to the handful of reapers that had gone off the grid to join the rebels.

The war had also pushed more stagnant reapers to enroll in extra classes, with hopes of learning something new that might help them defend their harvests in the event they became a target for the rebels. As the dean of the academy, it was up to Grace to figure out how to balance the scales. A tidy office was probably the least of her worries at this point.

"Ms. Harvey," Grace said, surprise hitching her voice as she looked up from her desk. She rolled her shoulders and straightened the green cardigan hanging on her thin frame. "To what do I owe the pleasure?" she asked, pointing at an empty guest chair. Its mate was cluttered with a stack of folders weighed down by a rusty hole punch.

I squeezed past a file cabinet and sat down, clasping my hands together. "I need your help," I said, getting right to it. Grace was old enough to be annoyed by small talk, and I was smart enough not to insult her by feigning interest in the weather or her personal life.

"I'm listening." She folded her arms over her desk and locked her owlish eyes on mine.

"I was wondering if I could get a printout of all previous students of Paul Brom's soul hypnosis class. I'd like to compare their names to the list of rogue reapers and see if anyone matches up."

Grace tilted her head to one side and then twisted her chair around to face another file cabinet in the corner behind her desk. "Sure, I can do that. But I don't know how much help it will be. It's one of the academy's most popular classes."

"I've gotta start somewhere."

Grace opened a drawer and zipped her fingers across the tops of the compressed files inside, pausing when she found the one she was hunting for. It was a thick file, and my head swam at the notion of having to go through the entire thing. Thankfully, she pulled several pages and ran them through a desktop scanner, promptly handing me the copies it spit out.

"That's it?" I asked, my eyes skimming the list.

Grace's clipped laughter startled me. "That's nearly half the entire reaper population."

"I never took the class." I flipped to the second page of the list, pausing to look up when Grace laughed again.

"*You* didn't take a lot of classes." She pushed her horn-rimmed glasses up her nose. "Of course, Saul's lot always did seem to prefer experience over education."

My chest tightened at the mention of my late mentor. "Thank you for your help. I appreciate it." I stood to leave, and Grace followed me out of her office.

"I know about the pickle you're in with the council," she said, shooting a quick glance down the hall. "Saul was a good man, and I know he was a good mentor. Trust that what he taught you will see you through this." She pressed her lips together in a tight smile.

I nodded and rolled up the pages she'd printed out between my palms. "Thanks again."

I left the academy in a hurry, already knowing where my next stop would be. But first, I called Kevin's cellphone. It immediately went to voicemail. That was odd. I called Bub next.

"Our bags are packed. Is it time to skip town?" he asked, the tone of his voice only half-joking.

"Not just yet. The council is giving me a chance to prove myself first. Are you at the condo?"

"Indeed, I am. I just returned from the market with all the fixings for a romantic dinner—"

"Is Kevin there?" I asked, cramming the papers Grace had given me down into my messenger bag.

"I don't believe so, love. I thought he'd be out with you, helping with the detective work. Maybe he's running an errand?" Bub suggested.

"Yeah, maybe. I'll try him again later."

"Kiss, kiss," Bub said before hanging up.

I thought to ask him if the hounds were home a moment too late. Maybe Kevin had taken them for a walk. Either way, the crusade had to go on. I tucked my phone back into my pocket and headed for the boat impound.

Two names in particular caught my attention on the list Grace had given me: Karen Durst and Tasha Henry. I didn't know much about Karen, just that she'd been on the Lost Souls Unit with Craig Hogan and Miranda Giles, two reapers who had been ripped out of existence—Craig at my hands, and Miranda at Grim's.

The ability to *unexist* someone was another thing I'd shared with my former boss, and one I was guessing I'd kissed goodbye during Naledi's extraction, along with my soul vision. Even more so than the soul vision, the ability to remove someone from reality wasn't a talent I advertised, though the fact that no one seemed to remember the person on the receiving end of said talent made bragging a little pointless.

The second name on Grace's list, Tasha Henry, was one that made my blood boil. The last time I'd seen her had been in Alaska, just before Christmas. She had been there to sabotage a high-profile harvest I'd been assigned to, and she'd almost succeeded. Unfortunately, the harvest was still a total bust. Tasha hadn't been the only one there to steal Christmas.

The rogue reaper had snatched a coin right out of my hand and disappeared, leaving Gabriel and me stranded. We had to search through miles of snow and ice for a coin I'd lost during the chaos. I was almost hoping she was involved with the soul-trafficking ring just so I could pay her back.

Before joining the rebels, Tasha had shared a boat with Karen Durst. Jenni and I had already searched it once, at the end of last summer when Grim's brother Hypnos had gone missing. We had been hoping to find a lead on the slumbering god's whereabouts but didn't turn up anything useful. Still, I thought it was worth taking another look.

The boat impound was along the north shore of Limbo City, just to the west of the Three Fates Factory. It was a short walk from the academy, so I bypassed the travel booths, choosing instead to head up Tombstone Drive by foot. The exercise made me feel more productive.

I caught a glimpse of the Sea of Eternity, poking through the patch of evergreens that stretched behind the academy. The coast was more severe on the west side of the island. Steep cliffs lined the perimeter of the woods, dropping off into the rocky depths of the sea. It was as if a small slice of forest had been slapped on the map to keep Limbo City from looking too industrial.

On the opposite side of the road, across from the sliver of wilderness, buildings rose up to meet the sky. Reapers Tower stood above the others, marking the northwest corner of the city proper. Ivy grew up the blond brick exterior, tapering off near the rounded corner columns with their medieval, tower-like quality that the building had been named for.

The apartments were a step down from Holly House, but a step up from the Coexist Complex, where I'd lived before upgrading. I knew a few of the reapers who lived there, including Ellen Aries and Mira Hart, a medium-risk harvester of my own generation. If Kevin didn't come with me to Tartarus, Reapers Tower would be a good fit. Jenni could afford the condo at Holly House on her own now—not that she would have any need to, seeing as how little she bothered to come home anymore.

Just past Reapers Tower, the street bent at a sharp right angle, turning into Remembrance Lane. I followed it for another block until I reached Ghost Alley and then headed north again.

The trees crept back into view as the buildings grew smaller and spread farther apart. The businesses on this stretch, payday loan offices and used appliance stores mostly, had seen better days. Many of their windows were dark, *Closed* signs dangling from the front doors. I wondered if they would even bother to open at all today.

The souls accounted for a good chunk of the traffic through this area, being so close to the factory. That was the only reason a business would choose to set up shop in the otherwise crappy location, with its uneven sidewalks and cracked road that eventually dissolved into weed-choked gravel. This part of the city wasn't a highlight on the tourist map.

The smell of burnt oil hit my nostrils as the ground tilted downward, and the boat impound came into view. It filled the space between the northern coast and where the gravel finally lost its battle with the weeds. A dilapidated construction trailer that served as the main office squatted behind a twelve-foot-tall fence. The crooked chain-link formed a wide half-circle around the property, enclosing the trailer, a shack of a work-shop, and a dry storage building half full of random boats.

The fence didn't stop at the coast. It stretched out over the water on both sides, disappearing beneath the sea about ten yards out. One side connected to a rickety dock, and the other left enough space to form a narrow channel for boats to pass through to be hauled up a concrete ramp for storage. A rusty gate adorned with several locks closed off the gap, ensuring that no one could make off with a boat they hadn't made bail on yet.

I readjusted the strap of my bag over my shoulder and slowed my pace on the way down the slope, stepping around overgrown clumps of weeds and avoiding the mud puddles the rain had left behind. The evergreens that began behind the academy mingled with deciduous trees near the impound, including several massive varieties. Their canopies blotted out the sky, shadowing my path.

A distant giggle echoed through the trees, and I paused to look around. A few of the fey residents in Limbo City occupied the coastal woods, and their taste for trickery kept most other citizens away. I continued down the hill, quickening my stride as I neared the impound entrance.

The chain-link gate was unlocked, but I had to lift the latch with both hands and maneuver it open an inch at a time. The rusty hinges felt like someone had tried to weld them in place, and their noisy protest alerted Nik, the water spirit who managed the place.

The door of the trailer swung open, slapping against the outer wall, and Nik waddled down a stack of cinderblocks that served as stairs. A wooden pipe poked through his mangled, black beard, and green algae dotted his cheeks and arms. He dug his webbed fingers down in the bib pocket of his overalls and pulled out a wad of tobacco, stuffing it into the end of his pipe before retrieving a book of matches from another pocket.

"You got ma chicken?" he mumbled around the pipe before lighting it.

"What?" I gasped and gave the gate a final shove, opening it just enough to slip through.

"Ma chicken," Nik repeated, giving me a once-over and then glancing behind me with a frown.

I wiped my hands down the front of my jeans, smearing them with orange rust from the gate. "Why would I have your chicken?"

He sucked on his pipe and blew a stream of skunky smoke in my direction. It caught in my throat as I panted to catch my breath, and I gagged as I stepped back and waved my hand in the air.

"I'm here to look at a boat that was seized last fall," I said, giving him a sour look. "A yacht that belonged to a pair of reapers, Durst and Henry."

"I know it." He puffed on his pipe again and folded his arms over his belly. "Gonna take six hundred to release her, and fifty more to get her license up-to-date."

I shook my head. "I'm not here to claim the boat. I just need to search it for evidence."

"Evidence of what?" he asked, his bushy brows arching.

"That's council business." I gave him a tight smile. "How about you just point me in the right direction?"

"She's in the water," he said, turning away from me to lift the gate one-handed. He pulled it all the way open, the hinges moving effortlessly and without a single squeak. My eyes bulged.

"What the—?"

"Gonna have to wait a bit, though. Lunch'll be here any second." He glanced up at the road that ended at the top of the hill.

My stomach growled, and I remembered that I had skipped breakfast. I'd grab a quick bite as soon as I had a look at Tasha's yacht.

"I don't need an escort. Just tell me which slip it's in," I said, taking a few steps toward the dock.

"You don't wanna be doing that until ma chicken gets here. You need a biscuit."

I crinkled my nose at him. "Thanks, but I'm good."

"You a snake charmer?" He looked over his shoulder at me.

"What?" I put my hands on my hips and sighed.

Nik snorted. "I didn't think so." He looked back up at the road and grinned. "Here we are."

A demon on a bicycle wobbled down the rocky hillside. A paper sack dotted with grease sat in the wire basket attached to the handlebars, and the demon's eyes widened as he rolled over a big rock, and the sack bounced violently. He stopped and repositioned it in the basket before rubbing a handkerchief between the horns that ran in a row down the center of his head.

"Tick-tock, boy!" Nik shouted at him from the gate.

The demon put his feet back on the pedals and struggled down the rest of the path, his lips pressed together in a determined line.

When he reached us, Nik spat out his pipe and tucked it away in his pocket. Then he tore the bag out of the demon's basket. He removed an entire rotisserie chicken, clutching it in one hand. His lips stretched wide, splitting his face in half like a toad's. I watched in horror as he stuffed the entire chicken in his mouth, crunching once, twice, and then swallowing the thing whole.

My stomach churned again, less eagerly this time as if reversing its previous request.

Nik tossed the demon a coin and waved him off, closing up the trick gate behind him. He turned to me as he reached down in the deflated delivery sack, scraping his fingers along the bottom. "There it is." He pulled out a crumbly biscuit.

"Really, I'm fine," I said, placing a hand over my mouth and turning away before I gagged.

"It's not for you." Nik walked past me toward the dock. I followed him, eyeballing the boats as we neared. The sooner I looked at Tasha's yacht, the sooner I could get out of there and forget the grotesque meal I'd just witnessed.

We passed the workshop where a trailer was jacked up and waiting for new wheels. The dry storage building was on the other side of the lot. Boats of every size, style, and era were tucked away. I spotted a steamboat and an old Viking ship. Some had probably been there for centuries.

In addition to holding boats for missed payments or late dock slip fees, Nik was also known to take trade-ins and sell them on the side. Not that he had the first clue about the boat market. I mean, who had the disposable income to hire a team of oarsmen to run a Viking ship these days?

The impound dock was tethered to the shore by a wooden ramp. It stretched high over a section of water before arching steeply downward and latching onto the dock. The cables running under and around it suggested the thing broke apart in the middle so larger boats could pass through to the slips gated off on the other side. Before we'd made it halfway across, the sea grumbled below. The ramp swayed, and I grasped the railing just in time. A funnel of icy water gushed up around us, spraying between the weathered boards and assaulting us from all sides.

Nik placed one of his fishy hands over the pocket of his overalls to protect his tobacco. His other hand held tight to the biscuit, even when a giant-ass snake reared its ugly head and hissed in his face, fangs as long as my arms ready to strike. I suddenly wasn't sure if the liquid soaking my pants was *just* water.

CHAPTER ELEVEN

"The voyage of discovery is not in seeking new landscapes
but in having new eyes."
—*Marcel Proust*

Water dripped from the snake's fangs. It leaned in so close to Nik that I could see his bored expression reflected in the creature's eyes.

"Oh, shush," Nik said, lobbing the biscuit into the sea with as much care as I would have tossed a toy to one of the hounds.

The snake fell on the biscuit, sending up another tidal wave that thrashed the worn ramp and shook us about. Then the slithering monster sank back beneath the sea just as suddenly as it had risen. The water smoothed over as clear as glass, and if not for our drenched state, I would have been tempted to question whether it had happened at all.

I blinked stiffly and let go of the railing to finger back the wet curls sticking to my face. Then I gave my bag a shake, hoping the faux leather was water-resistant enough to keep my stuff from being ruined. My hands trembled, and my whole body began to shiver as the breeze whipped across the sea and coiled around the dock.

Nik squeezed the water from his tangled beard and laughed at me as he retrieved his pipe and filled it with tobacco again. "Don't worry. She ain't gonna ask for another one on the way out."

My breath felt cramped in my lungs, and I wasn't sure I wanted to test his theory. I wasn't sure I wanted to do anything besides go home and take a long, hot shower. This day just kept getting better.

"This way," Nik shouted, disappearing around the bow of a speedboat that jutted out over a good chunk of the dock walkway. I ran after him, not wanting to wait around and see if the snake would come back for seconds. How much could a biscuit really satiate a creature of that size?

Tasha and Karen's yacht was near the end of the dock, and it looked as if it hadn't been touched since Jenni and I last examined it. The door on the main deck had been reduced to a pile of splintered driftwood, thanks to Jenni's impatience and bad mood at the time. No one had bothered to board it up. The inside stairs that led up to the control room had been sealed off, so Jenni had kicked in the door on the second-tier deck, too. That opening was crisscrossed with yellow caution tape.

"Didn't get no keys for her," Nik said, scratching along his jawline and flicking water from his beard. "Don't think you'll need none to have a peek, though."

I nodded and glanced down between the dock and boat, scanning the shadowy water for any sign of the snake. Then I held my breath and leapt over the short distance.

"I'll be in the office if ya need me." Nik turned to walk away.

"Wait!" I reached a hand out toward him. "You can't leave me here alone with that thing on the loose."

"I done paid your toll. Haruna is a good girl. She won't bite you unless you try to make off with one of ma boats," Nik said without looking back. He waddled down the dock, leaving me frozen in place on the yacht deck.

My shivering grew worse, and I hugged myself as I looked around, trying to remember why I'd felt so certain this was such a good idea. Jenni and I hadn't found anything before, but her revenge mission and a pressing deadline from Grim hadn't allowed for a very thorough inspection.

I climbed up the stairs to the second tier. The lower level had been a soul holding room, so I doubted there would be anything important to discover. Plus, I wanted to put as much distance between myself and the water as possible.

I ducked and stepped through a gap in the caution tape. The upper-level room was quite a bit smaller than the soul hold, and the ceilings were lower. Short, wide windows spanned both the port and starboard walls, letting in just enough light for me to find my way around. An overturned chair lay in the center of the cabin. Cobwebs laced between its legs, as well as the legs of the desk against the port wall.

The two beds shoved up against the opposite wall were made up with musty, green blankets. I snorted, wondering if the new and improved Tasha, with her demon punk makeover, still took such care to tidy her bed.

I set my bag on the desk and rummaged through the drawers again, finding nothing more interesting than I had the first time. Then I walked over to one of the bunks and peeled the blankets back before flipping the mattress over to inspect the underside. I ran my fingers along the stitching, feeling for any hidden openings. Finding nothing, I propped the cushion against the back wall and knelt down to pat down the bedframe. It was boxy like a daybed, and with the mattress out of the way, I saw that it housed a long drawer.

My surprise was stunted by the fact that the drawer was empty. I dismantled the second bed and found its drawer empty, too. Disappointed, I flopped the mattress back into place. A rustling noise made me jump, and I almost climbed up the wall in fear that Nik's *pet* had sought me out.

I peeked around the bed and squinted at the shadows along the floor where the light coming through the windows didn't reach. My knee bumped the bedframe, and the sound came again.

I removed the mattress a second time and took a closer look at the empty drawer, kicking the front panel that had helped disguise it with the toe of my boot. The rustling noise grew louder as I pried the drawer open, jimmying it awkwardly from side to side until it slid away from the frame.

The floor beneath the drawer was bare. I ran my hand over the dusty boards, just to be sure my eyes weren't playing tricks on me, and then growled out a frustrated sigh before flipping the drawer upside down. A handful of crinkled pages were stuck to the bottom. Their edges were worn and curling under, and a piece of tape over one corner had popped free, likely the source of the noise.

I peeled away the tape from the other three corners and turned the papers over in my hands, hooting out a quiet victory cheer. Several of them proved to be a folded-up map of Limbo City. It was an older edition, lacking the travel booths that had been added to the newer maps sold to tourists and factory souls at the Limbo City Welcome Center.

Several spots on the map were marred by tiny burn holes as if someone had used a cigarette in place of a marker. It was hard to tell if the marks were accidental or on purpose. A few of the holes had been circled with something cakey and red. *Lipstick.*

I refolded the map and stuffed it down into my bag with Grace's list. Then I flipped through the remaining pages, hoping for something more useful. A scrap of paper slipped from the pile and fluttered toward the floor. I snatched it before it landed and held it up to the window for a better look.

It was a faded receipt—the generic kind that came from stores too cheap to have their business information stamped above the date and time. Which narrowed it down to maybe a hundred businesses in Limbo alone. Great. On the back, a phone number had been scribbled down in blue ink.

Aha! I internalized my excitement, realizing it was much too early for a victory dance. It could be a number for pizza delivery for all I knew, but the fact that it was taped up with all of the other documents made me think I was onto something. I needed to figure out who the number belonged to and what their connection was to Karen or Tasha.

I tucked the rest of the pages and receipt down inside my bag, deciding that I had found enough to give myself permission to get the hell out of there. I poked my head past the caution tape across the doorway and shot a nervous glance at the dock and water below. I set my back in a straight line and very quickly walked down the stairs, then hopped lightly onto the dock and made for the ramp.

I took care to stay perfectly centered on the walkway, tucking my arms in close to my body. I held my breath long after I'd reached the land, almost to the point of passing out, until I reached the shoddy little trailer Nik called his office. Only then did I glance back at the sea.

From the shadowy water beneath the ramp, two glossy orbs the size of basketballs observed me. I shuddered as I beat on the trailer door, quickly stepping back when it swung open.

"Ya find anything good?" Nik asked. He popped the pipe out of his mouth and licked his lips.

"Maybe. Think you could open up the gate for me?" I asked. My hands still hurt from my first attempt, and they were stained orange with rust.

Nik snorted and hobbled down the cinderblock steps again. A soft bubble sounded from the shoreline, and I looked back in time to see the black snake eyes sink below the surface of the sea.

"I think she likes ya," Nik said, leading the way to the gate.

"I think she'd like to eat my face off," I grumbled under my breath.

Nik laughed and pulled the gate open just as easily as he had the first time. "Gonna put that boat up for auction soon. I don't think those girls is ever coming to collect her—and even if they did, I suppose I'd have to report them to the authorities." He scratched at his beard and tilted his head to one side. "But I guess there ain't no rule saying I can't take their money first." He gave me an obnoxious grin, his lips stretching unnaturally wide and showing off his tobacco-stained teeth.

"None that I'm aware of," I said, stepping around him and through the gate.

"See ya 'round," he hollered as I made my way up the hill.

The gravel dust stuck to my boots and the hem of my jeans. With my hair drying to my face, and smeared rust on my hands and clothes, I looked like hell by the time I reached the blacktop road. There wasn't much more damage I could do until I cleaned myself up.

I hooked a left and headed up Factory Bend Road, hoping I'd reach the travel booth up the way before the souls began returning from their lunch break at the factory—if they were even allowed to leave for lunch without a nephilim escort. Walking through the city looking like a vagrant was so not happening, even if it was more deserted than usual.

CHAPTER TWELVE

*"Change is the essence of life. Be willing to surrender
what you are for what you could become."*
—Reinhold Niebuhr

I opened the front door of the condo to find Kevin standing in front of the refrigerator, sniffing at the leftover tomato soup Bub had made for me the night before.

"Put. It. Back," I snarled.

His eyes bulged, and he quickly obeyed, opting instead for a bag of carrots and a container of French onion dip.

I slid my messenger bag across the table, leaving a sticky trail of brine. A kitchen towel draped over one of the barstools caught my eye, but then I thought of Holly Spirit's goading comment from the morning meeting and decided I really didn't care if I left a few water stains behind. They'd go nicely with the hellhound shit on the rug. And maybe a pair of socks in the garbage disposal.

"What happened?" Kevin asked as he peeled open the container of dip.

"I think I found something."

"Better you than me." One side of his mouth twisted up as he scrunched his nose at my appearance.

I kicked off my boots and glared at him. "Where were you this morning? I tried to call."

Kevin bit into a carrot before answering. "I went for a run in the park. Didn't know how long your meeting would last."

"Well, it's over now. You can round up the troops while I take a quick shower."

"What troops?" He stopped chewing, and I could tell that he was thinking of Josie by the way his eyes glazed over. He blinked a few times and cleared his throat.

"Abe, Jenni…Bub," I added, though I wasn't really sure if the Lord of the Flies counted. Jenni wouldn't want him involved, and I didn't feel right asking him to stick his neck out for the jerks who'd almost left him to rot behind enemy lines. But his eyes were too good to not at least have him take a look at what I'd discovered.

Kevin licked a smear of French onion off his lower lip. "I don't have Abe's number."

"Then call Ross. He'll have it. God, do I have to think of everything?" I stormed off toward my room, but he hollered after me.

"And Jenni never answers her phone when I call. Maybe you should—"

"Ellen," I shouted before slamming my door.

Coreen lifted her muzzle from the bed and sniffed at the helljack puppies tucked in against her belly. Then she gave me a dirty look as if I'd nearly woken them.

"Whatever," I hissed at her. "The only sound that stirs them is kibble."

One of the puppies' ears twitched, earning me another glare. The little beasts were far too big for her to be coddling them the way she did. It surprised me coming from Coreen, the more reserved and disciplined of my hounds. Saul was probably hiding out under Kevin's bed so he could get some quality naptime in.

I grabbed a fresh pair of jeans from my dresser and a gray sweater from the closet. The chill of the sea hadn't left me, and I could feel it settling into my bones. Add in the nagging doubt that the map and other scraps of paper I'd found would yield anything useful, and my mood was quickly degrading. I knew it wouldn't take long for everyone to arrive, so I hurried, skipping makeup and not bothering to dry my hair after I'd showered.

When I came back into the kitchen, Bub waited on one of the barstools at the breakfast bar. A bowl of steaming tomato soup sat before him, and he sipped it daintily from a spoon.

"I tried to tell him." Kevin held up his hands.

"The chef always gets a free pass," Bub said, patting a napkin to his mouth before leaning over for a kiss from me. My chaste peck was met with a displeased grunt.

"Hope you left some for me." I turned away to open the refrigerator door. "I'm so hungry I could eat a—" My mind flashed to Nik and the entire chicken he'd devoured. "Bowl of soup," I finished awkwardly as I spotted the plastic tub. There was just enough left for one.

Kevin gave me a quizzical look as I fixed my bowl and popped it into the microwave. He'd moved on from the carrots and dip and now snacked on a bag of chips.

"So, what's this Kevin says you've discovered?" Bub asked, pushing his chair back. He crossed an ankle over his opposite knee and rested an elbow on the counter.

I went to the kitchen table where my messenger bag sat in a salty puddle and dug out the folded map. The edges were damp, and the ink bled through in places, but it was still in decent enough shape to work with.

I moved the box of files into one of the dining chairs and laid out the map, spreading it across the side of the table that wasn't wet. Kevin stepped in beside me and ran a towel over the mess I'd made. I let him, not yet ready to have the conversation about my upcoming move to Tartarus and the sabotage plans I had for the condo.

"Did you get ahold of Abe and Jenni?" I asked my apprentice instead.

He nodded. "Abe should be here soon, and Ellen said she'd tell Jenni as soon as her meeting with the Fates was over."

Bub tapped the end of his cane on a corner of the map as he joined us at the table. "I certainly hope the scorching happened before this came into your possession," he said, frowning at the burn holes scattered across the page.

"Yeah." I pointed out the lipstick circles. "And I think the marks were deliberate."

Kevin hunched over the map. "Isn't that where the apartment building was that you and Jenni burned down last summer?"

He frowned at one of the larger smudges of lipstick. The burn hole was pretty big, consuming most of the outline of a building. It wasn't labeled, but it was on the right street and block. Jenni would probably have a better idea. Surely, she had taken the same, boring History of Limbo City class that Josie had gone on and on about.

Bub poked his finger down at another smear of lipstick along the southwest edge of the island. "This one is the abandoned resort. It was deemed off-limits after—" He gave me a tense smile and touched my shoulder.

It was still unpleasant to think about the day I'd discovered his involvement with the rebels. The fact that he hadn't told me before going undercover and that he'd paraded around with a succubus to gain the rebels' trust didn't do much for me either. It also chafed that the demonic harlot was still on the loose. I'd been too worried about Bub's near-death condition to give chase when I exchanged Winston for his freedom.

I pushed the past out of my mind and focused on the map. It was doubtful that Tasha had updated the thing since she was outed as a rebel. The apartment fire and resort raid hadn't happened yet, so the lipstick couldn't signify compromised safe houses.

I redirected my attention to the smaller burn holes. There was one over Purgatory Lounge, and another in the park. I couldn't name the others, but there were at least two dozen.

Bub's lips stretched into a worried line. "Is this all you found?"

"No," I said defensively, shoving my hand back into the messenger bag to retrieve the crumpled receipt. Bub sighed and gave me a withering look.

The doorbell rang out a series of hymnal notes, cutting off my would-be reply. Kevin left the table to answer it, snagging the bag of chips off the counter on his way.

Abe greeted us with a nod as he stepped inside the condo. He looked a little unkempt in his wrinkly white tee shirt and faded jeans, and his worn work boots made me rethink my earlier assumption about his post-guard occupation. The circles under his eyes suggested our gathering had interrupted his regular sleep schedule, and he didn't look happy about it.

I pointed him to a chair on the opposite side of the table and then stopped Kevin before he sat down again. "Why don't you start up a pot of coffee?"

Kevin huffed under his breath, but he didn't say anything as he circled the breakfast bar and began digging out all the coffee fixings. Playing barista was a poor substitute for harvesting souls, but I hoped a little detective work would be more to his liking.

Abe's wings fluttered, and his brow seemed to unfurrow a bit as the coffeemaker hissed and the smell of dark roast drifted over to the table. "Where did this come from?" he asked, nodding down at the map.

"It was hidden in a pair of rebel reapers' abandoned watercraft. Jenni and I overlooked it before." I turned the page around so he could read the street names and the few land markers that were actually labeled. The rest required a more thorough knowledge of Limbo City's structure than I possessed.

Abe squinted at the map, his eyes falling briefly on each burn mark, lingering longer on the ones circled with lipstick. He dug his cellphone out of his pants pocket and held it over the table, pausing to give me a questioning look. "May I—?"

I shrugged. "Yeah, sure."

Abe clicked a few buttons on his phone, and then a beam of light projected over the table. It spread out to reveal a modern map of the city, although more finely detailed than the ones found in the tourist shops. It was probably issued to him through the Guard. He moved his phone up and down until the streets lined up, revealing the building names near each of the burn marks.

I snagged a notebook out of my messenger bag and circled the table to sit beside him, quickly scribbling down addresses and business names. Kevin had been right about the burned-down apartment complex. A black box filled the square outline on Abe's light-up map. The burn hole had been blotted out, but the lipstick circle was still visible.

The caption under the box showed that it was the former location of the RIP Apartments. I didn't remember seeing anything specifying the building's name when Jenni and I had paid Tasha's demon ex a visit there at the end of last summer. Of course, most of the apartments on the west side were run by slumlord demons or defunct deities who couldn't even be bothered to keep up with building safety codes. And who needed to invest in proper signage when you could buy a three-dollar yard sign to advertise your vacancies?

I pointed at the black box marking the remains of the apartments and then at the abandoned resort along the southern coast. "We can skip these two. The apartments are gone, and the resort is more heavily patrolled now." I decided to skip over the whys of each and cleared my throat. "We still have five other locations that Tasha marked more specifically—"

"How do you know it was Tasha?" Kevin asked, passing out mugs of coffee. "Didn't she share her boat with Karen Durst?"

I pointed at the black box on the map again. "An old boyfriend of hers lived there."

"Is that really enough to draw conclusions from?" Abe turned off the light on his phone and set it on the table before stretching his shoulders.

"He's quite right, love," Bub said. "Don't let your anger at her besting you last winter paint her as every new villain. It might hinder your investigation."

I could feel my face warm with annoyance. Kevin didn't say anything, but his eyebrows lifted with alarm, and he made an exaggerated point of looking down the end of his own nose as he took a drink of his coffee.

"She didn't best me," I said through gritted teeth. "And it doesn't matter whether the map is Tasha's or Karen's. They're both on the lam, and this is all we have to go on at the moment. Do you any of you have a better idea?" I was on the verge of shouting, and from the silence and everyone's guarded expressions, I could tell they knew it, too.

Abe drained his cup of coffee and set it down on the table hard—harder than he intended if the surprised flutter of his wings were any indication. "I don't have guard duty tonight, so tell me where to go and what to look for."

I exhaled slowly as I refocused on the map, trying to relax the strain I could feel creasing my face. "You can have the Phantom Café. Take Tasha's and Karen's pictures from the most wanted database and show them around. Then check out the market booths. I know the vendors change too regularly to keep up with on a map, but it's worth taking a look."

"What about me?" Bub asked. "I want to help."

I shook my head. "Jenni would kill me if I let you get involved. The council may have pardoned you, but they're a long way from trusting you, even after Cindy's reluctant confession."

"I'll go in disguise," he insisted. "Or I can just casually walk by and take a look. They don't have to know I went there on your orders. Let me help."

I chewed my bottom lip and sighed. "There's the grocery store over on Westwood Drive—"

"I'll take it," Kevin snapped, blushing when I gave him a pointed look. "We need more coffee and milk anyway. Two birds, one stone."

"What about this one?" Bub asked, pointing at a spot near the condo.

"I know the owner," I lied. "I'll take that one."

He frowned, much as I had at Kevin, and then scanned the map for the final lipstick smudge. "That leaves…Saint Benny Jo's, the thrift store." He gave me an appalled scowl. "I can't go in there. I wouldn't be caught dead in secondhand rags. All of Eternity knows that."

"Caught dead." Kevin snorted. "Most of Benny's customers *are* dead."

I rolled my eyes. "I have a bag of old clothes in my closet that I've been meaning to donate for a while now. You can drop it off for me and save yourself the embarrassment of looking like you're there to shop."

Bub didn't seem to like that idea any better, but then his eyes lit up. "Do you suppose the receipt you found could be from the thrift store?"

"It's possible. We'd need another one to compare it with to be sure."

His face crumpled again. "That would require me to actually *buy* something, wouldn't it?"

Kevin slapped him on the back as he stood. "You sacrificed most of your wealth and good reputation last year to take on an undercover mission, and now you're worried about being seen making a cheap clothing purchase?"

Bub shrugged. "Everyone has their limits. Besides, being evil is much more believable of me than being cheap."

Abe stood and rubbed his hands together as he rotated his shoulders. "Looks like we're all set. Think I could get a cup of that joe to go?" he asked, eyeing his empty mug.

CHAPTER 13

"I think to be in exile is a curse, and you need to turn it into a blessing. You've been thrown into exile to die, really, to silence you so that your voice cannot come home. And so my whole life has been dedicated to saying, I will not be silenced."
—Ariel Dorfman

I followed Bub, Kevin, and Abe across Memorial Drive to the travel booth on the corner, where I gave Bub a quick kiss and bid them all farewell as they ventured off to investigate the locations Tasha had circled on the map. I was still determined that it was hers.

Maybe Bub was right. Perhaps I had painted Tasha as the villain prematurely, but I didn't care. She was already guilty, so even if her lipstick didn't match the circles on the map, it wouldn't do anything to help her case in my book.

Once I was alone, I crossed Divine Boulevard and stopped in front of the Little Folk Shoppe. The heady smell of incense created an exotic haze that stretched down the sidewalk in both directions and stained everything a pale gray.

I'd almost given the store to Bub to check and saved him from his own personal nightmare, but nostalgia had stopped me. Winston used to sneak out of the throne realm to buy Naledi incense from this quaint little shop run by an exiled faerie, and we'd held secret meetings in the tiny garden tucked between the shop and the alley out back. I'd never actually been inside before.

The store's front door was painted dark brown, looking much like a tree trunk against the building's flaking, green brick exterior, and even more so with the narrow arbor that framed the door and supported a tangle of honeysuckle. It was so overgrown that I had to duck when I entered.

I expected a bell to jingle, but instead, the corner of the door bumped a wooden wind chime suspended from the ceiling. It bounced off the one hanging next to it, and then a domino effect took over, echoing an endless encore of hollow knocks and thumps.

"Be with ye in a moment," an aged voice called from somewhere unseen.

I closed the door behind me and took a cautious step inside, avoiding the many tables of trinkets that crowded the entry. Rows and rows of short shelves filled the small space, and over their tops, I spied a pair of curtains that had been tied off to reveal a window into a small back room.

As I neared, I noticed a counter spanning beneath the curtains, topped with an old-fashioned cash register and a dozen mason jars filled with various stones and crystals. One of the containers held some water and several blackthorn clippings heavy with white, star-shaped blossoms. I couldn't smell them over the musk of incense, but they were beautiful to look at. So beautiful that I didn't notice the little old man until he was standing right in front of me.

"What can I help ye with today?" he asked, giving me a tight-lipped smile. It seemed more of a polite effort to hide his unusually sharp teeth than a show of unwilling cheer. I'd caught a glimpse when he first spoke, and the oddity compelled me to look for more.

I quickly noted his pointy ears and the extra knuckles on his spindly fingers. His arms were curiously long, as well, leading me to believe that his dress shirt was custom-stitched to keep from looking ridiculously ill-fitting. He seemed to care a great deal about his appearance, considering the crisp bowtie and polished Oxfords he wore. It was strange for his brand of fey, but the exiled did seem to have a more prominent human streak than their kosher kin.

I took too long to answer, and his friendly shopkeeper facade wavered.

"I'm just looking," I said, pasting on an awkward smile in hopes of bringing his back.

"So it seems." Unfiltered suspicion filled his dark eyes, but his smile returned, even if a bit tighter than before. "I'll be at the counter if ye find yourself in need of assistance."

I nodded my thanks as he turned and headed back toward a doorway that I guessed circled around to the spot behind the counter. When I saw him climb atop a stool behind the register, I ducked down one of the center aisles and pretended to check out all the random wares—chipped figurines, hand-woven baskets, dried herbs, decaying books with leather covers so scarred that the titles were no longer legible.

I tried to picture Tasha in here, perusing the aisles, finger-ing the useless trinkets. What made this place so special? Why would she circle it with lipstick on her map?

It was possible that it was just a meeting place. The old fey didn't look like the type to concern himself with the day-to-day turmoil of the outside city, and the garden out back had been secluded enough for Winston and me. Maybe it had worked for her, too.

A familiar smell gave me pause as I rounded the next aisle. Dozens of angled baskets were fastened together, each of them crammed full of incense cones and sticks. The con-trasting fragrances overwhelmed my nose. I took a step back and coughed into the bend of my elbow, and then took more shallow breaths through my mouth as I approached the aisle again.

It took longer than expected, but I eventually found the spicy frankincense and myrrh blend that Naledi preferred. It had just a hint of African violet mixed in, offsetting the strong musk with a delicate floral note. I took an empty wooden box from an opposite shelf and filled it with the black cones. There was no way I'd burn them in the condo—Bub was al-lergic to the exorcising properties of both frankincense and myrrh—but I couldn't leave without buying something. The old fey's beady eyes hadn't left me since he'd perched behind the counter. I didn't need him alerting Tasha if they were somehow in league.

"Find everything ye were looking for?" he asked crypti-cally.

"Yup." I gave him the box of incense and a pair of coins that covered my bill. He rang me up, dropping my coins into his vintage register before bagging the container of incense.

"Good day," he said, his wary eyes still trying to read me.

"You, too." I headed for the door, ready for some fresh air.

Once outside, I quickly stepped around the side of the building, circling to the back garden where I hoped to find something more useful. Any trace of Tasha would do. I just needed something to keep my spirits from dissolving completely.

Spring had done a number on the garden. It was even lusher than I remembered, as if winter had done nothing to slow its progress. A hedge of thick blackthorn bushes blocked off the view of the alley. The reach of their thorny, blooming limbs left only a narrow passage to access the dumpsters hidden behind a stone wall that blocked off the view of Memorial Drive. Baskets of daisies and petunias hung from the gothic spears that lined the top of the wall, making the space look like it had been transported here from a different time—if not for the occasional sound of a boat or car in the distance.

I sat my shopping bag down and bent over to check the weathered bench near the back door, running my hand under the seat and behind the backrest, feeling for anything that might be hidden there. Then I peeked behind the hanging baskets and under the various potted plants.

The back door creaked open suddenly, and the shopkeeper stepped out onto the patio, a black staff held tightly in his gangly fingers as if he expected to have to use it on me.

I held my hands up and backed away slowly. "I was just admiring your garden."

"Admiring me garden, eh?" he said, his Irish accent thickening with his anger and mistrust. "Ye be admiring the undersides of me patio stones next?"

I nodded at the buckets of flowers and plants lining the base of the stone wall. "I was just hoping to find a potter's stamp so I could purchase some of those for my own garden."

His eyes narrowed, and he made a jabbing motion as he took a step closer, backing me away from the patio and dangerously close to the blackthorn bushes. "And the hanging baskets? I suppose ye like those too, then."

"I do," I said, nodding vigorously. "You have the loveliest garden in Limbo City. Did you grow it all yourself?"

His cheeks flushed at the compliment, and I tried to hide my sigh of relief as he rested the foot of the staff on the ground. "Most of it. I hired a girl to fetch me supplies. She built the wall, too. Me old bones aren't cut out for such things."

"Did this girl have a name?" I asked. "I might like to hire her myself," I added when his eyes turned suspicious again.

"Sorry, lass. We kept our names and instead exchanged labor for goods and a place to rest until her work was done. She looked a lot like you." His eyes softened thoughtfully. "I've not seen her in some months now."

"That's a shame. I suppose I'll have to find someone else to help with my garden."

He nodded sadly. "I'd volunteer, but I don't stray far from home." His eyes migrated over my shoulder and toward the blackthorn hedge. I finally put my finger on his species. *Lunantisidhe*, guardians of the crone's sacred tree.

"I should really be on my way." I pointed at my shopping bag sitting near his feet. "Do you mind if I—?"

He glanced down and looped his staff through the handles of the bag, handing it to me from a safe distance. His mistrust had been muted but certainly not eradicated.

"Thanks," I said, giving him a small wave as I took the bag and slipped away, circling the building again and jaywalking across the intersection to get to Holly House quicker.

I still didn't know where Tasha was. But now I knew where she'd been, and it was a little too close to home for my liking.

CHAPTER FOURTEEN

*"Only enemies speak the truth; friends and lovers lie
endlessly, caught in the web of duty."
—Stephen King*

I busied myself at the condo as I waited for the others to arrive. I brewed more coffee and fed the hounds. Then I ordered a pizza. My bowl of tomato soup had been forgotten in the microwave, an unappealing film forming over the surface. Now, I was really starving, even when recalling the image of Nik and his chicken.

Bub was the first to return after I did, and I wasn't at all surprised.

"Anything?" I asked before he'd even closed the front door.

He gave me a dejected sigh and tossed a shopping bag on the table. "A Hawaiian shirt that smells like it was peeled off a man who died in a public restroom." Then he dug the receipt I'd found out of one pocket and the new one he'd just acquired out of his other, holding them side by side for me to see. "I'm afraid it was all for nothing."

I lifted an eyebrow. "Hold up." I found my shopping bag from the Little Folk Shoppe and dug out my receipt for the incense. It was a perfect match, and I was willing to bet that the phone number scrawled on the back was to the store, as well.

"That's one mystery solved, at least. Did you learn anything else while you were there?" Bub asked.

"Tasha apparently did some work on the back garden in exchange for food and a place to sleep for a few nights. Almost got myself brained over that tidbit of info."

"You're sure it was Tasha? Wait—I thought you said you knew the owner." Bub gasped in horror. "You naughty girl. You sent me to that store on purpose. The stench of mothballs and mildew is still clinging to me like rancid cologne." He pinched the shoulders of his dress shirt and shook it in my direction to prove his point.

I cringed apologetically and leaned over to give him a kiss on the cheek. "I still love you, no matter what you smell like."

The doorbell rang, and I turned to answer it. My stomach grumbled, happily anticipating the pizza guy, but it was just Abe. One of his cheeks was smeared with something sticky and white. I made a face and pointed.

"Yeah, yeah," he said, rubbing his jaw against his sleeve. "I was assaulted with a sticky bun at the café."

"Mm-hmm. I hope you found out something useful during snack time."

Abe glared at me. "One of Maggie's waitresses plays softball on the seraph league. She's one hell of a pitcher, and she didn't care much for my snooping," he added when I gave him a confused look. "But I think I know why the café might be appealing to a rebel." He handed me a photocopy of the café's employee schedule.

"What's this for?" I asked, not recognizing any of the names penciled in on the calendar.

Abe tapped a sticky finger on the page, leaving a dot of frosting behind. "Maggie's got a blind cherub working for her. Bet he can't tell a reaper from a troll."

That meant Tasha might still be using the café during the cherub's shifts. My pulse danced excitedly.

"Good work." I patted Abe on the back and folded up the schedule, tucking it down inside my messenger bag for safekeeping. "Did you find anything at the market?"

Abe's pride flat-lined. "Sorry, with so many of the booths shut down, it was hard to accomplish much. Some of the vendors have bespelled security systems. One of the dock guards is still laid up at Meng's after getting a face full of brimstone-shot for investigating a noise coming from one of the tents about a week ago."

I laughed dryly. "Bespelled security system? That sounds more like a booby-trap. Whose tent did it come from?"

Abe shrugged and rubbed at his cheek again. "Don't know. The guard's partner found him in the middle of the street and called for backup. Took two days for him to even remember his own name. We checked all the tents the next morning when the vendors arrived, but nothing turned up, and no one claimed responsibility."

Bub and I exchanged a look, and then we both turned our heads to look at Saul curled up on the living room rug. The hound could track a week-old scent through hell and a den full of sweaty demons—and he had. Jenni could vouch for that. I wondered if he'd be able to sniff out the brimstone remnants after all the rain we'd had. It was worth a shot.

The doorbell rang again, and my stomach growled with less cheer this time, demanding to be fed. The smell of garlic and melty cheese filled the condo as I opened the door. The delivery guy was a saint—literally—though one of the minor ones who had relocated to the city with visions of grandeur. Pizza delivery probably hadn't been part of his initial plan, but the lure of Limbo City often found newcomers working part-time shit jobs to make ends meet.

I handed him a hefty coin and snatched the box, my hunger so intense that I almost slammed the door in his face. I impressed myself by waiting the few seconds until he turned to leave. Then I dropped the box on the table and flipped the lid back, snagging up a wedge loaded with all the fixings and taking a bite before the cheese even had a chance to separate from the rest of the pizza.

"I love it when she's ravenous." Bub smirked at Abe's wide eyes.

"Anyone hear from Kevin?" I asked around my mouthful of pizza. Abe shook his head, and Bub frowned as he took a peek at his cellphone.

"Maybe he recalled a few more things we needed from the grocer?" Bub suggested. "I did tell him to keep his mitts off the goodies I purchased for dinner tonight—if you still have an appetite by then," he added as I shoved the rest of my slice of pizza into my mouth.

I nodded and licked my fingers clean. "What about Jenni? Any word from her?"

"Nada," Abe said.

Bub shrugged. "I imagine the council is keeping her extra busy." He opened his mouth as if he wanted to say more, but then shot a quick glance at Abe and decided not to.

Keys jingled at the front door, announcing Kevin's late arrival. He entered the condo with a black eye that had clearly not been delivered via pastry.

Abe let out a startled laugh. "You win."

I put down my second slice of pizza and went to the freezer to grab a bag of frozen peas. "Hope this means you have good news for us," I said, pulling out a chair at the table for him before pressing the bag to his face.

He sucked in a pained breath and took the bag from me before sitting down. "I've got nothing."

"Then what the hell happened to your face?"

Kevin gave me a wounded look. "I ran into an old *friend,* and they tried to sell me something I don't buy anymore."

My fists clenched involuntarily, fingernails biting into my palms. "Sonofabitch. Do we need to pay someone a visit?" I asked, my mind jumping between going to Meng for a feel-good tea and tracking down the hellfire dealer for some pay-back.

Kevin shook his head, groaning when the bag of peas shifted. "No need. You should see the other guy." He gave me a weak smile, but then followed it up with a frown. "I didn't make it to the store. Sorry."

It seemed a little curious that it had taken him longer than the rest of us to make it back to the condo, and all he had to show for it was a shiner. I had the uneasy feeling that I was being lied to, and the thought that he might be using again pinched my heart with guilt.

I couldn't handle him having a relapse right now. I could be dead by the end of the week. I needed him on his game and by my side. And I definitely didn't have time to pencil in an intervention. Each excuse made me feel like an even worse mentor, so I let them ferment in my mouth unspoken.

I shrugged. "Bub and I can check it out later."

"Later?" Bub pouted. "But our dinner plans..."

"After we take Saul down to check out the market, we can do a late dinner. Have a slice of pizza if you need something to tide you over."

Bub's sulking was becoming less comical and more forlorn, tainting my guilt with outrage. What was wrong with everyone? Didn't they care that I was fighting for my life? I felt like I was doing a pretty good job keeping my panic in check, but damn, having to light a fire under everyone's ass was starting to do a number on my self-worth.

Abe yawned and stretched his wings. "You need me to stick around?" he asked, his eyes wandering over to the clock on the kitchen wall.

"No." I sighed. "Go get some sleep. We might need your help again tomorrow."

Abe gave us a half-hearted wave before ducking out the front door. I was almost angry with him too, but he barely knew me, and he'd cut sleep to offer his help. Bub balked about having to visit a thrift store and reschedule dinner.

"I'm going to change." I left the kitchen, heading back to my room with a building sense of urgency. I was going to find

Tasha and force her to reveal the ghost market, even if I had to do it all by myself. Then everyone could go eat crow.

CHAPTER FIFTEEN

"The woods are lovely, dark and deep.
But I have promises to keep, and miles to go before I sleep."
—Robert Frost

It was dusk before I made it to the market with Saul. Bub had come along too, though somewhat reluctantly after he realized I was angry with him. I was too focused on my mission to bother with a heart-to-heart right now, but that didn't mean my anxiety and hurt feelings weren't winding me up like a jack-in-the-box. I was hoping a new lead would distract me from my misery soon.

"Is everything all right, love?" Bub asked when Saul paused to poke his nose under a table skirt.

"Besides my swiftly approaching demise? Yup. Super-duper." I stopped in front of one of the few open booths and held up a picture of Tasha for the vendor, a blue-skinned djinn peddling knockoff wishing lamps. He shook his head slowly and then held a glossy lamp out to me. I waved him off and moved on down the street.

The market was still suffering from the soul scare, as evident by the numerous closed booths. Only four or five were open, though none of the vendors seemed to know anything more than what they'd already told the Guard a week ago.

Saul whimpered at my ankles. He'd been snuffling his way up and down Market Street, booth to booth, curb to curb, for over an hour now, and we'd found absolutely nothing. I was having a hard time accepting it.

"Love," Bub said, taking my elbow and turning me to face him. "You need to relax. Even if the council doesn't vote in your favor, I won't let anything happen to you." He ran his hands up and down my arms.

"I can't relax. People are counting on me. I need to find Tasha and Jai Ling and the other missing souls, and then, if I'm lucky, I can keep my head. Because as much as you want to tell me everything will be okay, you don't know that—" I gasped in a shuddering breath and lowered my voice, realizing that I was drawing unwelcome attention from bystanders. "You don't know that. I'm not a child to be appeased with false promises."

Bub's face flushed, and he swallowed hard. "I'm merely trying to be helpful. I hate seeing you so distressed."

"You want to be helpful? Then help me find Tasha."

His eyes narrowed as he found his resolve. "I can do that. For starters, I can assure you that we won't find her here. It's much too public, especially at this hour."

I turned away from him and stormed off. Saul trotted along beside me, his nose still close to the ground. He was just as determined to find something tonight as I was.

"Where are you going?" Bub called after me.

"The grocery store on Westwood," I shouted back. I was going to accomplish something tonight, even if it was just picking up a few groceries.

Bub widened his gait to catch up, leaning on his cane with a grimace once he had. Walking the whole five blocks down Morte Avenue sounded like a great way to blow off steam, and it would certainly force him to prove how much he actually wanted to help, but I didn't think I could stomach any more guilt. Instead, I passed the dock entrance where two nephilim stood guard and entered the travel booth closest to the harbor.

Bub looked relieved as he joined me and propped himself against the glass wall to give his bum leg a rest. I slotted a coin in the booth dashboard, and we were promptly deposited on the opposite side of the island.

The sky seemed darker, as if the trip had taken an hour rather than a few seconds. It was likely due to the shady trees that crested the ridged coast. They towered behind the buildings lining the west side of the street, creating a hollow of darkness that prompted the businesses there to turn their exterior lights on long before those across the way did. The grocery store was one of them.

Westwood Supermarket was spelled out in electric yellow above the automatic doors. Half of the boxy letters were burned out, and the remaining ones buzzed and hummed as if they were ready to follow suit. Wide, glass windows wrapped around the building, and the few that weren't boarded up or sloppily painted with the weekly specials overlooked a sad produce section.

Bub shuddered beside me. "There are dumpsters better off."

I sighed, wondering if we'd have enough time to swing by the grocery store near the park before they closed. The way this place looked, I was willing to bet that the canned goods were even expired.

Saul bayed suddenly, his volume all the more jarring in the silence. Then he took off down the road, heading south toward the surrounding woods. I gave chase until he dipped behind the trees, hesitating as I tried to recall where the fey territory ended.

Bub stumbled against me, catching himself with his cane just in time. "What are we waiting for?"

"The fey—"

"Play house in the northern woods. We're safe here."

I took a few steps and stopped again, drawing a frustrated grunt from Bub.

"What now?" he whispered harshly.

"That's the way to the abandoned resort." I glanced back at him, and our eyes met in the near dark, the gold flecks in his glowing softly. A shared anxiety uncoiled between us, but Bub was quick to dismiss it. He grabbed my hand and pulled me into the woods behind him.

The ground was soft from the recent rains, and dewy leaves brushed my face as we followed the sound of Saul's panting. He knew not to disturb prey when sneaking up on it. The bit of light slipping through the canopy caught on his shiny black fur, giving me a glimpse of him any time Bub sidestepped around a tree.

The ridge dissolved into a rocky beach, and the sound of waves rushing to shore filled my ears as we exited the forest.

The sea was nearing high tide for the evening, the soulish water creeping up near the skeleton of a rusty beach umbrella. The three run-down buildings that had once been an extravagant and ill-conceived resort loomed along the edge of the woods. Saul waited in the shadow of the first one, his nose to the ground and tail wagging.

Bub and I followed the tree line, trying to stay hidden while also avoiding the weedy undergrowth of the forest. My heart rattled furiously in my chest, and I felt my hand grow clammy in Bub's.

Following the rebel bust last year and the boat sighting between the shore and the synthetic defense reef, the Guard was supposed to patrol this area more diligently. This was *their* job. I didn't want to be here—especially not with Bub.

We reached Saul, and Bub leaned over to touch the earth where my hound's muzzle pointed. His fingers came away crusty and yellow.

"Brimstone powder," he said, looking up at me.

I dug a hunting knife out of the sheath built into the side of my boot and looked up the length of the building. "Lotta stairs. Maybe you should stay here while I check it out."

I'd been so hard-pressed to see proof that he cared, but now I couldn't bear the thought of being here with him again, as if it were the location that had caused him to betray me before and not something of his own doing.

Bub shook his head stiffly. "Not a chance." He flicked his thumb along the handle of his cane and a series of dark spikes sprouted along the base near the ground. "I know how to handle myself just fine, love. Besides—" He lifted his index finger close to my face so I could see the glossy, green-eyed fly perched on his nail. "Stairs have never been an issue."

I swallowed and nodded. Then I patted my hand against my thigh, signaling for Saul to resume the hunt.

We followed the hound to the backside of the building where several rusty dumpsters huddled around the rear entrance. It was less visible than the front and more appealing to squatters and delinquents. Either the doors hadn't been sealed up last fall, or they'd been breached again recently. One was jarred open, and the smell of mold rolled out to greet us.

Saul slipped inside first, and Bub and I followed through the narrow gap, mindful of the old hinges that were sure to creak if we forced them. The fading daylight did little to light our path, but luckily, we didn't have to worry about playing truth or dare with the rotting stairs leading up to the next floor.

Saul led us through the foyer and to a pair of swinging doors off an area that looked like it might have been for fine dining at one time. A few round tables lay on their sides, propped together against a wall and covered with a stained tablecloth as if a hobo had built himself a little shelter in case the ceiling collapsed. Part of it already had, and fresh water damage was eating away at the rest.

Bub edged past me and peeked through one of the oval windows of the swinging doors. He jerked away suddenly and waved his hand at me, directing me to press myself against the wall beside him.

"Tasha?" I whispered.

Bub shook his head. "Demon."

My shoulders sagged, and my breath rushed out with less care. All this buildup, all this tension and heartache, for some random demon.

"He could still know something useful," Bub hissed under his breath as if I were ruining a perfectly good heist.

"Fine." I stepped around him and pushed the doors open, ditching stealth and opting for a surprise party explosion of noise. One of the swinging doors slammed into a cart, sending it hurtling into a stainless steel counter and adding a nice touch to my approach. Bub clicked his tongue and sighed before following me into the kitchen.

The demon in question cowered near a walk-in freezer. He balled himself into a corner on the floor, holding his arms up over his head as he pleaded for mercy. Saul growled low in his throat, and the poor guy pissed himself, making me feel more than a little depraved.

"*Manto*," I ordered Saul, freezing him in place so the demon could pull himself together.

He was a small creature with thin, webbed wings that shuddered in time with each heaving breath he took. The way he shrank away from confrontation made me think that there was no way he was—or ever had been—associated with the rebels. His clothes were ratty and stained, and it was hard not to feel sorry for him. Until I caught sight of his disfigured hand.

"Tack!" I tangled both hands in the front of his shirt and pulled him upright.

"I didn't do it," he wailed, holding his fingerless hand in front of his face.

Bub's eyebrows shot up. "You know this fellow?"

"Where's Tasha?" I demanded, ignoring Bub's question. "Where the hell is Tasha?"

"I don't know. I don't know." He choked out a strangled sob and shook his head from side to side, his wings flapping against the wall as if he were a bug trying to escape.

Saul growled again, and Tack squealed in my grasp, his wings pulling him off the floor a few inches. I held firm to the front of his shirt and pulled him back down, pinning him in place against the wall.

"I will rip those wings off and let my hound use them as chew toys if you don't tell me where she is."

"I don't know. I don't know," he began chanting again.

"Okay, then." I placed a hand on each of his shoulders and twisted him around, slamming his face against the wall.

"Wait! Wait. Sometimes, we meet up at the Phantom Café. She might be there later." His breath rushed out desperately.

"Why do you meet her there? Are you helping plan an attack on the city?" Bub asked.

"No, no. She buys me coffee and a bagel. Makes sure I'm doing all right." His voice broke, and he squeezed his eyes shut. "We aren't hurting anyone. She doesn't even deal with the rebels anymore."

"Why is she still in the city? What is she planning?" I shouted, pressing him harder against the wall. Adrenaline coursed through my body with a vengeance, and I couldn't contain my wrath. Tack cried out in pain.

"Lana." Bub placed a hand on my arm, urging me to release the demon before I crushed the poor guy like a cockroach. "We have a solid lead. Let's call the Guard in to collect him."

I held on a second longer, contemplating whether or not we might be able to get more information. My body trembled, and I finally let go, dropping Tack to the floor again. I took a deep breath and backed away, letting Bub take over while I dialed Abe.

He answered on the third ring, his words groggy and edged with frustration. "The world had better be ending."

"Not on my watch."

"Captain Harvey?" He cleared his throat, and I heard the squeak of a cheap mattress in the background. "Has there been a new development?"

"I need you to come by the abandoned resort and pick up a demon we're detaining. Bub and I would bring him in ourselves, but I'm afraid our new lead will expire soon." I closed my eyes and squeezed the bridge of my nose as a headache wrapped itself around my temples.

"Be there in five," Abe said, hanging up without another word.

I scuffed the toe of my boot along the grimy linoleum and glanced back at Bub. His hand rested on the demon's back. He was talking to him in a hushed voice, saying soothing things, promising no harm would come to him if he cooperated. Tack still quivered under my gaze, but his blubbering subsided.

"You're one of them that destroyed my apartment. One of them that did this," he accused, holding up his fingerless hand. "Aren't you?" His fear boiled into anger.

I flinched when Bub's astonished eyes sought me out. He didn't say anything, but I could imagine the conversation we'd likely be having later.

"We were looking for Tasha and her rebel companions then, too," I said as if that explained everything. My cheeks warmed, shame spoiling my feeble victory. "If you'd answered Jenni's questions the first time, she would have let you keep your fingers. But if I remember correctly, you were more interested in filling your veins with hellfire. I'm surprised you made it out alive."

"No thanks to you." Tack pulled his hand back in against his chest. His face crumpled with regret. "Tasha set me up at the Demon Suffrage Shelter. They had healers and rehab programs."

"I thought she left you for one of the rebels." I raised an eyebrow.

"She did," he snapped. "But it didn't last. She felt bad about putting me in the middle of all her drama. That's why she checks up on me every now and then."

"Why not stay at the shelter?" Bub asked.

Tack snorted. "Have you seen it lately? After the attack on the city last fall, anyone who shows up at the shelter is treated like a rebel refugee. They ask too many questions, and my visa is expired."

"Why not go home then?" I asked, making a face at Bub when he glared at me.

"He wouldn't last one night in any of the hells. Not in his condition."

A swoosh of wings echoed through the foyer, followed by a screech of metal as the back door was forced open.

"Hello?" Abe called out.

"In here." I put a hand on Tack's shoulder and led him out through the swinging kitchen doors. Bub was right behind us, the end of his cane making a ripping noise as it peeled away from the sticky floor.

"Where should I take him?" Abe asked as he bound Tack's hands beneath his twitchy bat wings.

"The Nephilim Guard station seems as good a place as any. Then call Jenni—"

Tack jerked around to look at me over his shoulder. "The reaper who maimed me? Are you serious?"

I silenced him with a glare. "Tell her he needs to be fed, but not to question him until I get there."

Abe nodded and led Tack away. I waited until I heard him take flight outside, his wings plenty strong enough to support the emaciated demon. Then I turned to face Bub.

His melancholic eyes searched mine. "The only thing that poor boy is guilty of is loving a bad apple." He tilted his head to one side. "Am I guilty of that, too?"

I blew out an offended breath. "I didn't cut off his fingers. That was Jenni. If he'd given her the answers we needed sooner, it wouldn't have come to that."

"Right," Bub said softly. "Do you suppose it would have come to that if he'd been an angel? Or a nephilim? What about a reaper?"

I took a step toward Bub and lowered my voice. "I'll do much worse when I find Tasha."

I thought of Craig Hogan and the way my hand had melted through his chest. Yeah, I didn't have a problem smiting my own kind when they deserved it. It might haunt me later, but my survival instincts didn't much care about the consequences.

Bub clicked his tongue and walked past me. "Vendettas don't suit you, love."

CHAPTER SIXTEEN

*"I'm tired of fighting.
I've always known that I can't be an action star all my life."*
—Jackie Chan

A long row of attached, three-story buildings filled the entire southern stretch of Eternity Avenue between Destiny Avenue and Memorial Drive. When the buildings were brand new, in the late eighteen hundreds, the gray block had been seamless, making the attached buildings look as if they were one. Almost like a very large, majestic library.

After a few decades, the businesses that had taken up shop there began updating and customizing. A candy-striped awning here. A new door there. Maybe some obnoxiously bright paint to stand out from the neighbors. By the end of the nineteenth century, every building had acquired a new look, each strikingly different, like carnival booths crammed together down a midway. The businesses they housed were just as varied, but the loft apartments on the second and third floors of most of the buildings still maintained a certain uniformity that I was pretty sure hadn't been updated since the eighteen hundreds.

Discreet alcoves were cut into the stonework where one building met the next. Their doors opened into narrow foyers featuring antique mailboxes and rusty, ominous heating grates that groaned and rattled when the furnaces kicked on. Rickety wooden stairs led up to the second and third floors, connected by landings with massive, arched windows that had outlived their weathered bench sills.

It was on one such bench that Bub and I staked out the Phantom Café, spying it through the dusty window while we avoided looking at each other or talking. Saul lay against the wall beneath us, his soft snores echoing through the stairwell. I pulled my legs up, letting my boots rest on the span of bench between Bub and me, and folded my arms across my knees. It was late, much too late for Bub's romantic dinner plans. I had the feeling neither of us was in the mood anyway.

The café didn't see much traffic on Monday nights, but my eyes never strayed far from the front door. Sammy, the blind cherub, was working behind the counter, and through the wraparound walls of glass, I counted exactly three customers. A dozen more had come and gone, taking their coffees and pastries to go.

A soft mist began to fall, fogging the window and the street below. Zibel was at it again. I rubbed the sleeve of my sweater across the glass and squinted at the sidewalk below.

Bub glanced at his watch. "How much longer do you suppose we'll be here?"

"You're free to leave whenever you want."

"That's not what I meant." He sighed and hefted a leg up on the bench, resting his booted foot between mine. "When are you going to tell me what's really bothering you?"

I pressed my lips together and gave him a sideways glance. "You mean the death threat hanging over my head isn't enough?"

"Why are you letting this council business get to you? You didn't give a flip about what they thought last fall when you put your neck on their chopping block to save my arse."

"That was different." I leaned my forehead against the window, letting the cool glass soothe my disappointment. "I had no choice."

Bub's hand rubbed up the side of my calf. His fingers found mine, and they laced together. "You had a choice, and you have one now."

I swallowed and turned my gaze back to the café. "You had a choice too."

Bub's grip tightened. "I did, and I made the wrong call. I'm done jumping through the council's hoops, love."

"You really think that's an option for me?"

"I'm not telling you to give up," he said gently. "Just don't let them lead you around by your fear. If you don't complete this mission, we'll leave the city. In my time with the rebels, I learned quite a lot about the hidden nooks and crannies of Eternity."

I looked away from the window again. "We'd have to give up the new manor."

"It's just a house. It means nothing without you." He pulled my hand to his mouth and brushed his lips against my knuckles.

My heart fluttered, and I felt tears sting my eyes. Maybe he'd made the wrong call going undercover with the rebels, but I hadn't made a wrong call saving him without Grim or the council's approval. I'd do it all again, and they knew it. That's why they were punishing me now.

Something unclenched in my chest, and I realized I'd been reading Bub all wrong. He did care—enough that the council's verdict wouldn't change where he saw us in the future. Together. Whether that be among the mortals or in a far-reaching corner of Eternity. That's why he wasn't as worked up over this whole ordeal as I was.

Bub was right. I was letting the council get to me. I had my allies, but there were too many uncertain variables. Sure, I wanted to get Tasha back for her hijinks over Christmas, and I most definitely wanted to save Jai Ling. Being able to show my face in the city and go about life as usual sounded nice, too. But fear of death still had top billing on my motivation list. It didn't render a very courageous or optimistic outlook.

"Hello there," Bub said, leaning closer to the window.

A slender figure wearing full black and stilettoed boots hurried down the sidewalk. Her face was hidden under the hood of her sweatshirt, but I caught a glimpse as she twisted her head about, making a quick assessment of her surroundings, and then pushed through the café's front door.

"That's her," I whispered. Saul snorted and yawned as he lifted his head. He stood and shook out his coat before extending his front paws and leaning back into his haunches for a good stretch.

I stood too and paced back and forth across the landing.

Bub arched a brow. "Shouldn't we go get her now?"

I shook my head. "We're going to follow her, see if she leads us to anyone else who might know something about the ghost market. That way, we have something more to work with if she decides not to talk."

Bub smirked. "You don't think she'll spill her guts if you have Jenni chop-chop?" He brought one hand down in a slicing motion over his opposite fingers.

I shrugged. "Maybe. But she's a little tougher nut to crack than her ex. Still, I'm not letting her get away this time."

"In that case, we better move." He nodded down at the sidewalk as Tasha left the café.

"Come on." I took off down the stairs, leaving him and Saul to trail after me. A swarm of flies buzzed past my cheek, and Bub materialized in the lobby half a floor ahead of me. He lifted a closed fist for a bump when I reached him, as if I'd won a prize for taking second place—Saul was still plodding down the stairs behind me.

"We don't have time for games," I said, tapping his closed hand anyway. His fingers uncurled theatrically, releasing a tiny fly.

"There's always time for games." He grinned and cracked open the lobby door, letting the fly slip away to begin scouting for us.

"That won't work for long. It's going to rain."

"We'll catch up in time." Bub offered me his arm, and we walked outside together, following Tasha's trail at a leisurely pace. Saul nosed the ground at our feet. I hoped he could pick up her scent before Bub's fly-cam called it quits.

Thunder grumbled in the distance, but every time I tried to quicken our stride, Bub would pause to window shop. He'd point out a jewelry display, a concert flyer, a blooming tree growing up out of a cutout in the sidewalk. When he stopped to buy a bag of popcorn from a street vendor, I'd had my fill.

"Are you *trying* to sabotage my mission?" I hissed under my breath as we neared the travel booth on the corner of Destiny Avenue.

"She's already two blocks ahead." Bub wiped a dribble of butter off his bottom lip with his thumb and licked it clean. "I thought she might be going back to the resort, but she hasn't taken to the woods yet. Perhaps she's heading to the grocery store on Westwood? That was on her map, was it not?"

A drop of rain hit my cheek, and I gasped. "We're going to lose her."

Bub tossed another piece of popcorn into his mouth and grinned. His cane was casually looped over one arm, but he removed it to hook around my arm as I took an angry step away from him.

"We'll use the travel booths and beat her there," he said, pulling me in line with him.

The nephilim ahead of us tucked his wings in tighter against his back, eyeing Saul as he sniffed his sandaled feet. He entered the booth quickly when his turn came, giving us a dirty look as he dropped a coin in place.

Bub grimaced. "It seems that stealth and notoriety don't play well together. Your little friend would have made us for sure if we'd blood-hounded our way through the city."

Saul snorted in offense, and I reached down to scritch him behind an ear. "It's not you, it's us."

When we popped out on the far side of the island, the sky looked fit to drench the city. Fat drops of water pelted the travel booth glass, and the fluorescent light overhead flickered like a beacon.

"Ah, yes, so much better. She'll definitely not see us coming now." I gave Bub a cheerless smile as he polished off his popcorn, crumpling the bag and shoving it into his pocket. Then he pulled me out of the booth and across the street, bypassing the automatic doors of the grocery store and heading straight into the western woods.

They were too dark for my taste, the only light coming from a yellow bulb set in a rusty, caged fixture at the store's rear. It barely lit the exit and dumpster it was intended for.

As we moved deeper into the woods, my skin crawled, every little hair standing up on end when a cricket chirped somewhere nearby. My breath hurt in my lungs, less from our roaming, and more out of panic. Bub was sure the fey gathered only in the north, but secluded bits of wilderness just seemed too tempting. I thought I heard voices, but when I hushed Bub to listen closer, there were only the crickets, occasionally drowned out by a roll of thunder.

The soft earth sucked at my boots, and I cringed when a thorny sapling scraped along my thigh, tearing at my jeans. I couldn't make out Saul's black fur in the darkness, but I heard his panting breath as he ventured ahead.

Bub was having an easier time navigating than I was, as well. His cane was looped over his arm again to save it from the muck, and he used the abundant tree trunks to pull himself through the thicker patches of shrubs and over exposed tree roots.

Once we were well out of sight, Bub stopped and pushed my back against a thick tree. His hips rubbed against mine as he trapped me there, planting a wet kiss on my mouth and then another on my neck. "She's almost here," he whispered breathlessly.

I twisted around to peer through the trees, focusing on the point where Westwood met Eternity Avenue. The streetlights had come on, but many of the businesses were closed by now, their darkened storefronts surrendering to the shadows.

A streak of lightning shot overhead like a comet, lighting up the clouds and reflecting off the damp streets. And then rain fell from the sky as if it were being poured from a giant bucket. My hair unfurled and clung to my face, and my clothes soaked through in seconds. Then, just as suddenly, it was over.

A break in the thunder left a silence so thick I could hear my own pulse—and the *click-click-click* of stilettos swiftly approaching.

Tasha looked perfectly dry, as if she'd taken shelter just in time. She passed the grocery store entrance on the same side we had and headed around to the back of the building, stopping beside the dumpster. She pulled her hood back, and the yellow security light spilled across her face like jaundice.

From the cover of the trees, I was finally able to take a good look at her. A lot had changed since Christmas. Tasha's mohawk had grown out, though it was still longer on top and mussed in such a way that suggested she cared more about staying off the radar than keeping up with her demon rebel makeover. Two tiny scars were visible where I knew she had dimples when she smiled. Apparently, she had decided the piercings drew too much attention, though she'd kept the row of studs in her left ear.

An owl hooted, and Bub and I ducked behind our tree as Tasha turned to inspect the woods. We waited to look again until we heard the lid of the dumpster creak open.

Tasha stretched her arms and tugged her fingerless gloves down before taking hold of the dumpster's lip and heaving it closer to the back steps. She climbed up the steps and leaned over to rummage around the garbage without having to actually dumpster dive. A pair of questionable apples went in the wide pocket of her hoodie, followed by a dented box of snack cakes.

Bub snorted softly in my ear. "*Bon appétit.*"

I elbowed him as Tasha stole another glance into the woods, and we hid behind the tree again. When we looked next, she was gone, the dumpster left open and the smell of rot filling the humid air.

"Shit." I tromped through the woods toward the grocery store, hoping to catch a glimpse of where she'd gone.

Bub was a few steps behind me when I came into the clearing. I glanced out at the street, scanning the shadows and listening for the clicking of Tasha's heels.

I didn't think to look behind the dumpster. Not until I smelled brimstone and felt the barrel of a gun press against the back of my skull.

CHAPTER SEVENTEEN

*"Natural selection, as it has operated in human history,
favors not only the clever but the murderous."*
—Barbara Ehrenreich

Tasha smirked. "You would have made a lousy rebel, you know that?"

"Well, there goes my weekend plans." I lifted my hands slowly and turned around to face her—or the barrel of her gun anyway. "Shoot anyone with that lately?" I asked, thinking of the guard still laid up at Meng's.

Tasha's scarred dimples flattened as her smile faded. "Only idiots like you who can't mind their own business."

"Yeah, who do they think they are, interfering with your thieving?" I leaned back as her gun drew closer to my face.

"I'm a little short on options, you may have noticed," she said bitterly, nodding her head back at the dumpster.

"And whose fault is that?"

Tasha's eyes narrowed, and I bit my tongue, remembering what end of the pistol I was on.

"Why are you following me?" she snapped. "Isn't patrolling the city the Nephilim Guard's job?"

"You mentioned the ghost market last winter when you tried to botch my harvest, remember?"

"So?"

"So, I'd like to know where it is."

Tasha rolled her eyes. "Trust me, precious. You don't want to get mixed up in all that."

"Tell me where I can find it, and I'll forget I saw you."

She cocked her head to one side and laughed. "Or I could shoot you in the head, and then you'd definitely forget you saw me."

A swarm of flies pelted Tasha's face then, buzzing in her ears and eyes. The brimstone pistol fell from her hand, and she covered her head, shrieking as she hunched over. Saul leapt from the dark cover of the woods and pounced on her back, sending her the rest of the way to the ground just as Bub appeared.

"Well, that was the wrong thing to say." Bub snatched up Tasha's gun with two fingers and held it up for inspection. "You won't be needing this any longer," he said, tucking it into one of the deep pockets of his coat.

Tasha's squealing curdled into a dry heave that sounded like she was having an asthma attack. Saul's weight against her back probably didn't help, but I had a feeling it hurt less than a bullet in my head would have.

"Let's try this again." I squatted down and leaned over so she could see my face from her flattened vantage point. "The ghost market. Where is it?"

"How should I know?" She grunted and squirmed against the cracked concrete. "I haven't dealt with them in months. They kept undercutting my commission, so it wasn't worth my time anyway."

"But you *have* dealt with them. Where?"

"They move around, you idiot. You think they'd still be in business if they weren't mobile?"

"You're going to tell us every location you know of—"

"Or what?" she said through clenched teeth. "You're going to have Toto here stomp me to death? How do I know you're not going to do that anyway? I'm not saying *shit*."

"I guess we could head back to Reapers Inc. and have him stomp Tack to death first. Maybe you'll talk then."

Tasha's eyes widened at the mention of her ex. She struggled harder against Saul, kicking the ground, and then went still. "Whatever. You don't have Tack." It was almost a question.

So she had an Achilles' heel, after all. I should have known. Why else would she risk being spotted in the city just to buy him a bagel and coffee?

"I'm curious why you're digging your dinner out of the dumpster—" I said as I stood and motioned for Saul to release her. Bub took one of Tasha's arms, and I grabbed the other, hauling her to her feet. "When you've got the coin to buy a homeless demon the good stuff from the café."

Tasha's face blanched, and her arm went slack in my grasp. She didn't say anything as we escorted her across the street to the travel booth. I had the feeling she would have walked there on her own if it meant making sure Tack was okay.

Something about that unwavering loyalty felt familiar, and as evil as Tasha might be, I still felt dirty for using it against her.

CHAPTER EIGHTEEN

"I think all of us have a hero and a villain in us."
—*Anson Mount*

The seventieth floor of the Reapers Inc. skyscraper had been remodeled to serve as the Nephilim Guard's station. The project began while Grim was still in office, but it had only just finished a few months ago. It would have been completed sooner, but the attack on the city had presented some setbacks. The construction crews were called away to attend to more pressing repairs first—like the damage done to the historic district near the harbor.

The dove gray walls and speckled tile made for a much cheerier environment than the thirty-seventh floor, and for the first time ever, I was a little disappointed by that fact. I had a feeling that the horror film set where Grim used to do his dirty work would have made things move along much faster with Tasha.

Instead, Ross had placed her in a starkly lit interrogation room. Tack was down the hall in one of the tiny, bland cells that featured a toilet and a cot chained to the wall. The room was so sterile, I was sure his hygiene was improving just by sitting in there. Someone had changed the dressing on his hand, and a nameless guard informed me that he'd eaten almost his own weight in bean soup and bread.

Bub had headed on home, taking Saul with him, so I sat by my lonesome on one of the vinyl-cushioned benches in the waiting area. A brand new vending machine hummed in one corner, and a shiny drinking fountain graced the opposite wall. The nephilim secretary, who looked very much like a winged version of Ellen, hummed while she clacked away on her keyboard, pausing every five minutes to ask if I was sure there wasn't anything she could get for me while I waited. She was certainly nicer to me than Ellen had been in quite some time.

Finally, Jenni arrived. She stepped off the elevator and crooked her finger at me as she headed toward Tasha's interrogation room. Ross spotted her through the glass window of his office and popped into the hallway as we passed by.

"Need any assistance?" he asked, his wings fluttering hopefully. The facility was so new, any chance to use it was met with gleeful anticipation.

Jenni shook her head. "Not just yet, but we'll let you know."

Ross frowned, but he nodded and watched as we disappeared inside the viewing room attached to Tasha's.

Jenni's stiff demeanor set me on edge. I hadn't expected a parade or anything, but something a little more congratulatory than the sour look she met me with didn't seem like such a tall order.

"Did you really have to bring the junkie demon in?" she whispered, her cheeks flushing with shame.

"He's clean now." I blinked stiffly. "Not that it matters. I brought him here because I didn't want him to alert Tasha that we were looking for her. And it's a good thing too, because I'm pretty sure he's the only way we're going to get her to talk."

I looked through the viewing window, startled to see Tasha staring right at me, her eyes unblinking and hands folded over the table. I moved a few steps to my left, but her eyes didn't follow, and I found I could breathe again.

Jenni took a deep breath and paced across the room, rubbing her hands up and down her arms. "You want to use the demon as a bargaining chip? Have Tasha reveal the location of the missing souls in exchange for his freedom?"

"Something like that." I shrugged. "What do you think?"

She pressed her lips together. "I think the council will expect a deal like that to be cleared through them."

I rolled my eyes. "Of course. Why wouldn't they?"

"Or maybe…" Jenni tapped a finger over her mouth thoughtfully. "Maybe we just don't lose any sleep over not keeping promises to traitors."

"Can we do that?" My stomach knotted. I wasn't very good at lying, and my moral compass had been dropped enough for one night. I wasn't sure it could take much more. I decided to rephrase the question. "Can *you* do that?"

Jenni sat down at the computer in the corner and clicked on the power button, lighting up the dark room. Her fingers moved lightly over the keyboard as if she were afraid someone might hear her typing. I read over her shoulder as a nervous energy took hold of me.

The contract promised immunity for Tasha and Tack if she helped us infiltrate and take down the powers that be behind the ghost market. It even stipulated that she would be reinstated at Reapers Inc. as a low-risk freelance harvester. I wasn't sure how Tasha would feel about that, but at least she wouldn't have to share her meals with rats and roaches anymore.

I chewed my fingernails as Jenni printed the contract.

"You really think that'll do it? She won't just run off the first chance she gets?" I asked.

Jenni bit her bottom lip. "I could call in a favor to be sure."

I gave her a puzzled look.

"Do you remember those bracelets you used last fall to track Winston and the original believers Naledi arranged her little treasure hunt with?"

My heart dropped. "Naledi told you about that?"

"Not Naledi." Jenni cringed.

"No. He's on the council. And there's no way he'd agree to what you're doing." I shook my head and turned away from her.

"What *we're* doing. Besides, we don't have to tell him everything," Jenni insisted. "We'll even let him hang onto the tracking compact. We'll just request the two bracelets."

Naledi must have removed hers, and I was pretty sure Winston's had been reclaimed before his memorial at sea. I didn't mention the other five I had stashed in my closet after Maalik forced me to give up the tracking compact. That small victory was still mine.

"Why do we need both of them? Who's the other one for?"

Jenni gave me a strained smile. "How do you expect Tasha to infiltrate the ghost market without a proper soul to pawn?"

"Good point." I blushed. "Uh, where exactly are we getting this proper soul from?"

"That's another favor." Jenni looked less thrilled about this one. "We're borrowing it from Asmodeus." She slipped out of the room before I could ask her for more details.

Asmodeus had been all googly-eyed over Jenni for a while now, ever since she'd come back from her week as a rebel captive, covered in blood and unconscious. For him, it was love at first sight from across the hall of Meng Po's temple, where they were both healing up after close calls with Caim, the rebel general who had met his gruesome end last summer when Jenni split him in half with her katana.

Jenni was having none of Asmodeus's courting—at least, not since the last time I checked. After Loki had pretended to be Apollo to woo her into a rebel trap, her love life had been nonexistent. I didn't blame her. Still, Asmodeus didn't give up easily. I had a pretty good idea what he wanted in return for this favor Jenni had called in.

Honestly, I was a little surprised at how much legwork Jenni had been doing behind my back. Of course, she wouldn't have her current position if not for me. Saving her from the clutches of the rebels was nothing to sneeze at either. It would have been nice—and also a little naïve—to think she'd done all of this out of the goodness of her heart, though.

If the council voted against me, it would set the stage for Ridwan to vote Jenni out of office, too. Bloodlust and power quests always seemed to have a snowball effect. It was too soon to be breeding chaos again. Eternity needed a break.

On the plus side, if the council did give me the eternal boot, at least I wouldn't be around to see them set the afterlife on fire.

I watched through the viewing window as the interrogation room door opened and Jenni stepped inside. She sat down across from Tasha and slid the contract and a pen across the table to her without a word.

Tasha read it silently and then picked up the pen. She glanced up at the viewing window again, narrowing her gaze as if she could see me watching her. It was unsettling, and something in her eyes suggested that she was well aware that I hadn't been the one to deliver the contract because I knew it was bullshit. She signed it anyway, but I didn't feel as relieved as I'd hoped I would.

I wondered if all villains felt this unsatisfied when planning to stab someone in the back.

CHAPTER NINETEEN

It was incredibly late before I made it home. Late enough that morning was already rearing its ugly head. Fortunately, the ghost market was a nocturnal creature, and Jenni didn't want to see me back in the office until Tuesday evening. Sleeping like the dead was at the top of my list for the day.

I wondered if that would be an option when I entered the condo to find Kevin in the kitchen, his hand pressed over the lid of the blender. The sound it made grated against my skull like a power drill, and the green goop spinning in the pitcher made my stomach turn.

"That looks like something you should be making in the bathroom. Ick." I made a face at him as I closed the front door behind me. "Why are you up so early?"

Kevin's jaw tensed, and he wouldn't look at me. "Apartment hunting."

I winced. "Oh."

"Gabriel stopped by last night, going off about Holly Spirit having a feather up her ass and how he was ready to put in his thirty-day notice, too." He opened the blender and dumped the questionable contents into a tall tumbler. "When were you going to tell me?"

"I've been meaning to. There's just a lot going on."

Kevin turned around and leaned against the counter, giving me a hurt scowl. His black eye was puffy, but I was glad to see that it hadn't swollen shut.

"I could have helped last night," he said. "Why didn't you take me with you on the stakeout?"

"I had Bub."

"Yeah, but I'm your apprentice. I thought I was going to be part of this new team. Or is that something else you've been meaning to talk to me about?"

I put a hand on my hip and glared at him. "I'd love to include you more, but you've been a little difficult to pin down since we left the Posies. You didn't pick up when I tried to call yesterday morning—"

"I told you, I went for a run."

"And you didn't even make it to the grocery store I asked you to check out, though you somehow took longer than the rest of us to return, and with a black eye."

Kevin set his cup down hard, splashing the counter with lumpy, mashed greens. "What exactly are you accusing me of, just to be clear?"

"What do you think?" I folded my arms, giving him a tired look.

Kevin pressed his lips together and nodded. He left the kitchen, coming back a moment later with a small, black box. He tossed it on the counter between us after he'd circled back to the blender.

"Open it," he said gruffly. "It's yours."

I snatched up the box and ripped the lid off, letting out a surprised gasp before I turned it upside down. The crystal bands my mentor had given me spilled into my hand. They'd been polished since I'd seen them last, presumably by whomever Kevin had hocked them to in order to buy a fix before he kicked his hellfire addiction.

I set the box aside and climbed onto a barstool to take a better look at them, running my fingers down the silvery strands to find all the familiar imperfections one notices after owning a piece of jewelry for a few centuries.

Kevin's face softened a bit. "Sorry it's taken me so long to track them down. I was going to wait until after this first mission was over, but not if it means you're going to think I fell off the wagon."

"I'm sorry, Kevin." I gave him a weak smile and then held up the crystal bands, watching them sparkle in the light. "Thank you."

"When are you giving Holly this notice?" He took a long drink of his concoction and leaned over the counter.

"After the council's ruling. I'm going to move into the new manor in Tartarus with Bub. It's almost finished."

Kevin nodded, making a painful face as he swallowed.

"What is that anyway?" I finally asked.

"Green protein shake. Ross says it'll heal up my eye faster."

I made a face. "And you believed him?"

Kevin shrugged and looked down in the cup at the remaining goop. "Maybe it's an acquired taste."

I shook my head. "Maybe you need better friends."

He grinned and gave me a teasing glare. "I've been wondering that same thing myself. So, do I get to play with the big kids today?"

"Tonight," I said sharply. "I haven't been to bed yet. Plus, our next operation won't be doable until nightfall. So, rest up, grasshopper."

I stood and circled the counter to give him a hug, pressing a kiss to the side of his head. "Thank you again, and sorry I doubted you."

Kevin nodded as he took another drink of his shake, but I wasn't sure if his grimace was protesting the flavor again or my affection. After Josie's death, he'd shied away from anything even remotely touchy-feely.

"See you at lunchtime?" I gathered up the jewelry box and tucked the crystal bands back inside.

Kevin nodded and then called after me as I stepped around the corner into the hallway. "You didn't happen to pick up any coffee from the store last night, did you?"

CHAPTER TWENTY

"If only I wasn't an atheist, I could get away with anything.
You'd just ask for forgiveness and then you'd be forgiven.
It sounds much better than having to live with guilt."
—Keira Knightley

"This does not count as a romantic dinner." Bub pouted over the box of tacos Kevin had picked up on his way home from touring the new duplexes going in on Divine Boulevard, near the road that led out to Meng's temple.

I moaned as I crunched through a beefy, cheesy taco and pressed my shoulder into Bub suggestively. "Is it romantic now?" I purred, though the effect was somewhat lost with a mouthful of food.

Kevin rolled his eyes and crammed the rest of his taco into his mouth, washing it down with a gulp of soda. His black eye was no better off than it had been that morning, and he'd clearly lost faith in the green protein malarkey Ross had tried to sell him on. Immediate results were hard to come by unless you were willing to choke down a cup of Meng's super tea, and I'd take a black eye over that any day.

Bub sighed as he fingered the wilty lettuce on his taco. "I have an organic chicken in the refrigerator. I bought fresh herbs grown in an enchanted meadow and harvested by pixies."

"Tomorrow." I crumpled up my taco wrapper and tossed it at the trash can. It bounced off the lid and hit the floor, where it was soon dogpiled by the helljack puppies.

They growled as they tug-of-warred the wrapper in half and then lapped up the traces of cheese and sour cream. The smaller of the two finished first and turned to nip at his brother's tail.

"Share, Tom." Kevin nudged the pup back with his foot.

"Tom?" I echoed with a snort. "You finally got around to naming them, and you chose *Tom*? Is the other one Garfield?"

"Felix," Kevin answered innocently.

"Those are cat names." I glared at him in disbelief. "You can't give puppies with jackal and hellhound blood cat names. It's just wrong."

Kevin shrugged. "Felix means lucky."

"I suppose that's why there are so many martyrs with the name." Bub smirked and pushed the box of tacos away.

"Really?" Kevin looked like he might be having second thoughts. "What about Blue and White? Like the two rivers that feed into the Nile. Get it?"

"Except the helljacks are both black," I said, standing up and dusting sprinkled cheese from my hands and pants. The puppies swarmed my ankles to scavenge.

"Well, what would you name them then?" Kevin grabbed another taco and unwrapped it with a frown.

"Gluttony and Wrath," Bub said under his breath.

Kevin rolled his eyes and took a bite of his taco, dribbling sauce down his chin.

I had hoped the lunch table talk would circle around to the possibility of Kevin moving to Tartarus with Bub and me, but every time it seemed like it might move in that direction, Bub had changed the subject.

Maybe he was just worried that we'd be on the lam and Kevin would be without a home if the council ruling didn't go my way. I couldn't handle that kind of doubt right now. It wasn't productive, and not everyone could forfeit their give-a-damn as easily as Bub. I needed a hopeful outlook if I was going to focus on what had to be done tonight.

"I've got some errands to run." I pulled on my boots and slipped my messenger bag strap over my head and across my chest.

"Want some company?" Kevin asked, wiping his hands down the front of his pants. He and Bub got along well enough, but my demon's melancholy was infecting the entire condo. Even Saul and Coreen looked depressed as they lounged in the living room, watching the puppies chase stray kibble under the kitchen table.

"I'm stopping by Athena's," I said, knowing the reaction I'd get.

Kevin blushed. "Uh, actually, I should probably take the hounds for a run." He cleared the trash from the counter and then went to dig the leads out of the coat closet. The slightly bigger helljack puppy slipped past him and pawed down the side of the Cerberus Chow food bag, spilling a handful of kibble.

Bub pointed his cane at the mess. "As far as suitable names go, I stand by my vote for Gluttony."

I laughed and gave him a kiss on the cheek before leaving the condo. Bub enjoyed shopping, but I needed an escape from his glum mood. I had enough guilt hanging around my head, so I refused to accept the blame for his sulking. There was nothing I could do about it anyway.

Jenni had said not to involve the Lord of the Flies. I'd gotten that lecture a second time after she finished making the phony deal with Tasha last night. But she didn't say I couldn't tell him what was going on.

I'd been extra forthcoming with the details, thanks to that pesky bout of guilt for not telling him about Naledi's procedure, and now I was kicking myself for it. Of course, he had to point out the underhandedness of our technique. And I'd known that he wouldn't like not being able to tag along, but the fact that Maalik was now involved made everything that much worse.

Fresh air and shopping, maybe a latte, that was sure to perk me up. It would have been nice to have a girlfriend along for the adventure, but I was in short supply these days. Josie had to go and die on me, Jenni was busy fighting for the title of ringleader within the council, and Ellen had been blowing me off with the excuse that Duster was newly resurrected and needed extra attention for the past three months. The amount of dust on her blouse Saturday morning proved that he'd been reborn much more recently, and it pained me that she had lied to avoid my company.

I sighed and hurried down the hall toward the elevators. Ever since I'd bumped into Holly, I'd been particularly mindful about coming and going. Her passive-aggressive attitude toward me lately was unnerving, especially when she'd been so eager to have me move into the condo in the first place. But, to be fair, that was two hounds, a demon, and some accidental bloodshed ago.

I rode an elevator down from the tenth floor and jumped when I heard my name as I stepped out into the lobby.

"Over here!" Warren waved his hand from the entrance to the parking garage. His wings fluttered excitedly as I approached him. "Well? How did it go?"

I tried to keep a neutral face as my pulse quickened. "How did what go?"

"Testing the gauntlet, of course." He gave me a forced smile and laughed nervously.

"Oh, man. Look, Warren. I haven't had a chance yet." I put a hand on his shoulder and sighed. "I promise I'll give it a go as soon as this mission is over. If I screw this up, the council is going to kill me." I didn't elaborate on the literalness of the statement.

Warren nodded, his smile looking more disappointed than hopeful. "I get it. I've botched a few things—but honestly, this is not one of them. You should really give it a chance."

"I will. Cross my heart." An elevator pinged behind me, and I glanced over my shoulder, blowing out a tense breath when I realized it was just my nephilim neighbor Harold.

I said goodbye to Warren and left Holly House as quickly as my feet would carry me. Athena's Boutique was only two blocks away, but even if I hadn't felt up to walking, there wasn't a travel booth any closer than that to her store.

The historic district had strict codes about new construction. The buildings were some of the oldest in Limbo, and they had been meticulously cared for through the centuries. When Grim began the travel booth project, the business owners on that stretch of Morte Avenue had put together a petition to prevent a booth from marring their perfect slice of antiquity. Athena's Boutique was smack-dab in the middle of that slice, the crown jewel of the new world beyond the grave.

The attack on the city had done the most damage down Morte Avenue, and another petition had ensured that their repairs received the most immediate attention. While Reapers Inc. was still being patched up more than six months after the fact, the historic district looked good as new.

The etched stone sign above Athena's shop had been washed clean by the recent rain, and ivy snaked its way over one corner and up the front of the building. A trio of animated, wooden mannequins pranced around in the display window below the sign, their arms linked together as if they were headed for the yellow brick road. They all sported slinky cocktail dresses and strappy heels.

One waved, and I lifted my arm to wave back before I could stop myself. My longing for female companionship was reaching pathetic new heights.

The bell above the door jingled when I stepped inside, and the smell of fruity perfume made my head spin. Racks of brightly colored clothes clashed together in a tropical jungle of retail euphoria. Several of the dummies on a central platform were lounging on beach chairs, plastic cocktail cups with tiny umbrellas in hand.

"Welcome to Athena's," a mildly bored voice said. Arachne hunched over the front counter, her nose pointed down at a magazine. "Please feel free to try on something from the exciting new spring line," she said in a dry monotone.

"Where's Athena?" I was surprised the goddess wasn't at her usual post behind the register.

Arachne glanced up and then back at her magazine. "On vacation. Can I take a message for you?"

"That's all right. I was just curious." My voice trailed off, and Arachne didn't bother acknowledging me again.

I stole a peek at her magazine and quickly realized it was the issue of *Limbo's Laundry* that I'd flipped through in Skipper's cab. She was reading the article about Naledi's new subcommittee. I was sure there were plenty of unflattering things about me in there, and I felt my cheeks warm as I turned away.

I pushed past all the bright colors and swatted away the hand of a mannequin as it tried to hand me a wide-brimmed sunhat, heading straight for the back of the store to the sole aisle of black garments. I found a pair of leather pants and a turtleneck, two items I had to replace in my wardrobe more often than seemed healthy or financially rational. The thought made the thrift store on Tasha's list come to mind.

I skipped the dressing rooms upstairs and headed straight
for the register, purchasing my items and leaving the boutique
before Arachne had read much more of her trash mag. I didn't
need the pomposity, and she didn't need the fat lip.

Benny Jo's was just north of the city park, close enough
to the factory to draw in the new souls with little to no disposable income. The patron saint of bachelors and beggars
seemed to give away more than he actually sold, a solid
enough reason for Tasha to lipstick him on her map, I guess.

Bub hadn't learned anything useful on his shopping ex-
cursion, but then again, saints didn't take too kindly to
demons poking around in their businesses. I was hoping I'd
have better luck.

I walked the three and a half blocks across town to the
quieter neighborhood and held my breath as I entered the
warehouse building through a glass door with peeling vinyl
letters. The smell of stale sweat and cheap air fresheners made
me want to run back to Athena's.

"What can I do you for?" Benny smiled at me from a
booth in the center of a sea of random castoffs. His eyes were
full of warmth, and he looked genuinely happy to be folding
the stack of tee shirts in his lap.

I set my bag from Athena's on the counter and dug Tasha's wanted flyer out of my messenger bag, unfolding it for
Benny to see. "Can you tell me when you last saw this reaper?"

Benny's smile froze in place, and he paused before shaking his head. "Sorry."

I slapped the flyer on the counter when he grabbed another tee shirt, forcing him to look up again. "I know she's

been in here. A lot. I didn't think saints were so prone to lying."

"I don't lie." Benny's voice remained cheerfully even. "I said 'sorry.' As in, sorry, but I won't be helping you."

I bit my bottom lip and sighed. "She's a rogue reaper who joined the rebels, a major threat to not only this city but all of Eternity. And you didn't report her to the Guard when she came into your store. I believe that makes you an accessory."

"To what crime?" Benny asked, his focus shifting back to his stack of shirts. "She never stole anything from me, and most of what she left here with was for others. What kind of saint would I be if I interfered with the good works of others?"

"Good works?" I shouted, earning a glare from a nephilim shopper on the opposite side of the store. "She shot a guard in the face with brimstone a week ago. He's still in recovery. How's that for good works?"

Benny paled, but he continued folding. "Let those without sin cast the first stone. Are you without sin?"

I left the thrift store in a fit of frustrated rage and stormed off down Destiny Avenue to the travel booth on Council Street. Good works, my ass. Tasha was probably taking the clothes across town and selling them to the thrift store near Westwood. Benny had totally been suckered. And just where the hell did he get off asking about my sins?

I decided to skip the latte because I wasn't sure I could handle anyone else telling me what a great person Tasha was. She was a traitor and a heathen, and if I didn't remember that, I was sure to regret it when she turned on me.

Not to mention, when it came time for me to turn on her.

CHAPTER TWENTY-ONE

*"It doesn't make sense to have to do the wrong thing
in order to do the right thing."*
—Jim DeMint

"It's…shiny," Bub said, admiring the silver cuff on my wrist. I'd finally broken down and dug Warren's new gadget out of the coat closet.

Kevin nodded in agreement. "Maybe too shiny. Doesn't really go with your ninja getup."

I tugged the arm of my turtleneck down, tucking the thin material under the edge of the device, and then went back to reading the instruction pamphlet.

"Eight-soul capacity, three-hour holding maximum, spring-loaded ejection lever under jewel casing. What the hell is that supposed to mean?" My eyes blurred as I tried to read the tiny print.

Bub snatched the pamphlet from me and held it under the chandelier over the dining room table. "I still don't see why I can't come along." He grumbled under his breath as he read and then reached for my hand.

I pulled my sleeve up again for him to inspect the gauntlet. "Jenni says the council will have a fit if you do."

"The council is a bunch of twats." He pressed down on a rounded cutout set along the rim of the gauntlet and a larger dome on the inside of my wrist popped open, revealing a dial. It pointed to the far left of a meter labeled one through eight, the color scheme shifting from green to yellow to red.

The cartoony nature of the inner workings clashed with the medieval exoskeleton, and it made me wonder if I was doing the right thing by wearing the gadget tonight.

"Maybe I should put it back…"

Kevin raised an eyebrow at me. "Warren will never stop harassing you if you do that. Just wear the thing around and tell him you're waiting for the right opportunity. At least that should back him off."

I tucked my shirt down over the gauntlet again and kissed Bub's pursed lips. I could only ignore his sulking at this point since there wasn't anything I could do to fix it, and he knew that just as well as I did. "I can't wait for that fancy dinner tomorrow night," I said, hoping it would lift his spirits.

"I'm eating that bloody chicken with or without you." He gave me a stern look.

"If it's going to be bloody, you might very well be eating it without me." I stuck out my tongue, smiling when he let a small laugh slip.

"Take care tonight, love," he said, his face falling somber again. "Don't put yourself in a pinch over those devils hiding in their ivory tower."

"At this point, I'm damned if I do, and damned if I don't." I shrugged. "It's an easier pill to swallow if I just think about saving Jai Ling." That was the only noble objective in this whole mission.

Kevin and I loaded up the battle gear and said goodnight, leaving Bub and the hounds behind. I wouldn't need Saul tonight, not with the tracking compact and bracelets Maalik was so *graciously* volunteering. And I didn't feel right taking Coreen away from her puppies since it was looking more and more like she would only have another month with them before the move to Tartarus—or wherever Bub and I ended up if the council tried to screw me over.

Abe was waiting for us at the Nephilim Guard station when we arrived. He'd swapped out his standard golden armor for a black set, and a black cloak topped the ensemble, hiding his white wings so he'd be able to disappear into the shadows with us.

Kevin tightened the strap of his bow over his shoulder. "Dude, you look like the Darth Vader of the Guard."

Abe made a face, but then looked down at himself and grinned. "I guess I do. I wonder if they'd let me trade my spear in for a lightsaber."

Chatter drifted down the hallway, and soon everyone else spilled into the lobby with us. Jenni led the way with Asmodeus close on her heels. A soul, the one I assumed we would be using as bait, followed a step behind.

Maalik brought up the rear, dragging Tasha along by her elbow. He frowned at the open tracking device in his other hand. "Everything appears to be in working order."

Tasha gave him a smug grin. "Well, that wasn't much of a test drive. And here I thought you were going to rev my engine and ride me around the block a few times." She gyrated her hips mockingly.

Maalik's face creased, and he let go of her arm. Tasha rubbed a hand over her opposite wrist. The tracking bracelets were a bit shocking in the way they dissolved under the flesh, invisible and undetectable without the tracking compact. Their technology was a bit dated and a teensy bit illegal—though not quite as illegal as being me, apparently.

The only time the bracelets had ever failed had been when Naledi manipulated the one I'd given her in order to lead me around Eternity to collect the original believers she'd found. I still wasn't sure how she managed it, but I figured it was one of the many perks of being the throne soul.

Jenni clapped her hands together to gather our attention, and we all huddled in a little closer. "Here's the deal. Ross and his men surveilled the known soul drop sites—"

"That *I* provided you with," Tasha interrupted.

Jenni gave her a lethal glare. "We've found one that looks fairly active over on Tombstone Drive. Tasha is going to take Ramone there and try to sell him."

The soul standing beside Asmodeus nodded, and Maalik squeezed his shoulder. The Keeper of Hellfire hadn't looked at me once, and I could tell he didn't like this plan one little bit. I wasn't sold on it yet either.

Jenni continued, "Then we'll track Ramone via the bracelet and hopefully get an idea of where the souls are being kept or how they're being transported out of the city. Once that's established, we'll send the Guard in to crash their party."

Maalik cleared his throat. "We'll be leaving Reapers Inc. in an SUV and escorting you to safe checkpoints since the travel booths are set to lock down if the facial recognition picks up Ms. Henry here," he said, nodding at Tasha.

"Why, thank you for that bit of information, Mr. Hellfire," Tasha said with a Southern drawl. "Much obliged."

"It won't do you any good," I said. "That bracelet can track you anywhere in Eternity. Unless you feel like chopping off your own, your ass is ours."

"Well, if you're so fond of my ass, why don't you go ahead and kiss it?"

"Focus, children." Jenni gave me a wide-eyed glare and straightened the hem of her blouse. "There are dozens of high-profile souls out there about to be traded into slavery. If you fuck this up, the council will have all of our heads on pikes by the end of the week. I wish that was an exaggeration but believe me when I say it's not."

My breath felt trapped in my throat, and I had to swallow before my lungs began working again. Jenni panicking was not a good sign. I wanted to ask her what had changed, but there wasn't time, and Tasha had been fed enough of my business for one night.

The smirk was gone from her face, but she still had that caged-animal look in her eyes. "Let's get this over with."

CHAPTER TWENTY-TWO

"The world is a fine place and worth the fighting for
and I hate very much to leave it."
—*Ernest Hemingway*

The drop took all of five minutes. It was neat and tidy, and something about it felt entirely off. The doorman at the site had taken the bait easily enough, but Tasha claimed that he had asked her to come back in two hours. Something about wanting time to appraise the soul's value.

So, we headed back to Reapers Inc. to watch the screen on the tracking compact, which was about as exciting as watching Saul take a dump after the time he'd foraged a whole block of moldy cheese out of the trash.

Abe and Kevin were stretched out over two of the vinyl benches in the waiting room at the Guard station, while Tasha and I occupied opposite ends of the one remaining bench, Maalik sandwiched between us with the compact held out for us to see.

Ross had given Jenni and Asmodeus his office for the night while he was out on patrol with his unit, and they'd disappeared in there shortly after our return, closing the blinds so we couldn't see them through the wide window behind the receptionist desk.

I checked my watch again, groaning when I realized we still had an hour to go.

"I'm hungry," Tasha whined, eyeballing the vending machine.

My stomach growled, agreeing with the wench against my will. The late-afternoon taco-fest hadn't been enough to carry me through the main event, but to be fair, I'd thought the world would be saved by now, and the plan was to celebrate with donuts or something equally sugary and fattening.

Maalik sighed. "The machine only takes tokens. I'll go see if I can find some. Keep your eyes on that," he said, handing me the compact.

Tasha watched him as he disappeared down the hallway and let out a lusty groan. "Mmm, I bet he's all muscle under that robe."

I felt my cheeks flush and crossed my legs away from her, angling the compact farther out of her reach. Her face held a taunting grin when she looked back at me.

"He's still got it bad for you, but you knew that already, huh?" Her eyes flickered down at the compact.

"Nice try, but really, even if you manage to get it away from me, do you think you'd survive the seventy-story drop once I throw you out the window?" I tilted my head thoughtfully and glanced out at the city lights, glowing softly behind our superimposed reflections.

Tasha snorted and leaned back on the bench, folding her hands behind her head. "If I have to stay here with you much longer, I'll save you the trouble and jump."

A silent moment passed in which everything was too loud—the drip of the water fountain, Kevin's snores, the clicking of Tasha's heels as she stretched her legs out over the tile floor. The blinking light on the compact hadn't moved, and I found that each second it remained stationary, my agitation grew worse.

"I paid your pal Benny a visit this afternoon," I said, having nothing better to do than make small talk with the traitorous fiend.

Tasha's head jerked up, but her expression was guarded. "Who?"

"Oh, come on. We found your stupid little map, and his store was circled in streetwalker-red."

"Sorry, don't know what you're talking about."

I turned to stare at her. "You know what else was circled with your cheap lipstick? Tack's apartment, the grocery store you get your takeout from, the booth at the market where you shot that guard—"

"That was an accident," she snapped, her face screwing up with rage. She took a deep breath and looked away from me, back to the window and our reflections. "I just needed somewhere dry to sleep, and the booths were closed. I wasn't there to hurt anyone."

My stomach clenched, but I credited it to my hunger. I refused to feel sorry for her. "Why not stay with Tack at the resort?"

She laughed like it was the dumbest thing she'd ever heard. "The Guard doesn't care if a homeless demon squats in one of those buildings. A lot of the nephilim were homeless squatters there themselves before they moved on up in the world. But a reaper at large?" She sighed. "Tack's been through enough because of me."

My stomach growled again. "Well, aren't you the saint."

"Did I ask you for a fucking medal?" Tasha glared at me.

"You joined the rebels. Do you really expect me to believe you give a shit about anyone but yourself?"

She considered me for a few awkward seconds as if she had a perfectly good explanation, but she thought I was too dense to understand it. Then she sighed and tilted her head back against the bench.

Maalik decided to return just then, and I glanced back down at the compact, making sure I hadn't missed anything.

"Found some," he said, waving a plastic baggie of green tokens. "What would you ladies like?"

Tasha turned back to me with a sneer. "Any last meal suggestions?"

Maalik raised an eyebrow and began pumping tokens into the vending machine, pressing buttons at random until he had a good variety of snacks. He gathered them up and deposited them on the seat between Tasha and me before reclaiming the tracking compact.

"Dibs on the peanuts," Kevin said. He sat up and rubbed the sleep from his eyes.

"I don't think so." Tasha snatched them up first. "All they serve here is bread and beans."

"Must be torture, I mean, given the fine dining you're used to." I grabbed a bag of chips and tossed it to Kevin, saving a candy bar for myself.

Tasha ignored me and tore open the bag of nuts, dumping them all in her mouth at once. She snagged a stick of beef jerky next and tucked a granola bar in her hoodie when she thought no one was looking.

As the two-hour mark drew near, everyone began shuffling around the room restlessly. According to the compact, the soul still hadn't moved. At one point, Maalik pulled me aside.

"What if it's malfunctioning again?" he whispered, giving me a worried look.

"Maybe that drop site is the main hub. Or maybe they haven't had a chance to appraise the soul yet," I suggested.

Maalik rubbed a hand down one side of his face, and his dusty wings bristled behind his shoulders. "Asmodeus and Peter both had big deliveries today, and three more missing souls have been reported—even with all of the extra precautions the Guard has taken."

I glanced past him to where Tasha was curled up on the bench. "Then I guess it's time for the guns-a-blazing part of the plan."

The clock on the wall showed it was nearing two in the morning. Maalik nudged Tasha awake as the alarm on Abe's watch went off, signaling it was go-time.

Kevin checked his quiver of arrows, while I grabbed my axe from where I'd propped it next to the water fountain. Abe fingered the end of his spear as if he thought it might have dulled since he'd last sharpened it, just before his nap.

Tasha watched us with bleary eyes and yawned. "Sure wish I had my brimstone pistol. Don't know how much good I'll be in a fight without it."

Abe gave her a hard look. "Guess we won't have to worry about *friendly* fire."

Tasha pressed her lips together. "Pretty easy to say you're gonna grant me immunity if you intend to send me into battle defenseless as a lamb."

"Here." I dug a can of angelica mace out of my pocket and tossed it at her.

"What the hell is this? Hairspray?" She gave me a belligerent scowl.

"It only works on demons, so you'll have to fend for yourself if we come across any of your deserter buddies, but it's better than nothing."

"I've always wanted to work in a demon salon," she said, her voice loaded with irony. "Now if I could just find a cursed curling iron, I'd be set!"

I pursed my lips. "If you don't want it—"

"I'll make do. Thanks, you're a peach," she said through gritted teeth. She stuffed the can into her pocket and stood, stretching down to touch her high-heeled toes. Her hoodie slipped up, and I noticed an angry scar curling around her waist. It hooked upward near the center of her lower back, disappearing under her sweater.

I looked away before she caught me staring. *Don't feel sorry for her.* It was going to end up being my mantra for the night. Because if I started feeling sorry for her, I was going to get the shaft. One way or another.

Maalik poked his head inside Ross's office to let Jenni and Asmodeus know we were on the move again, and then we packed ourselves inside an elevator car and took it down to the lobby.

Tasha pulled up the hood of her sweatshirt as we stepped out and headed for the garage exit. The building lights had been turned off for the night, leaving only the red glow of the exit signs. The giant front window was dotted with rain that had fallen while we waited upstairs, and the clean smell of spring reached all the way into the parking garage. I took several deep breaths, letting it fill my lungs before I crawled into the back of the waiting SUV.

Kevin and Tasha filed in after me, and Abe took the driver's seat behind the tinted windshield. I was surprised to see Maalik climb in with us this time.

"What Jenni doesn't know won't hurt her," he said, closing the door behind him.

Tasha gave me a sanctimonious grin as if to say that she had told me so and scooted over as Maalik took a seat beside her.

Abe pressed a radio button on the SUV's dash. "Ready when you are." He listened quietly to the replying static.

"All clear," a crackling voice said a few seconds later.

We turned east out of the garage onto Council Street and then cut down Ghost Alley. About a block from the drop site, we parked in a lot tucked behind a cluster of restaurants. The security lights were out, but I had a feeling that had been arranged by the Guard.

"You're up, Tasha," Maalik said, opening the side door. She gave him a hesitant frown. "Don't worry. We'll be right behind you."

Tasha snorted as if insulted that he was coddling her and then jumped out, slinking between the buildings and toward Tombstone Drive.

Maalik turned to me next. "You and I will come in from the south and watch the front. Kevin and Abe can take the north and come up on the backside."

"And here I thought I was captain of this unit." I raised an eyebrow at him and slung my axe over my shoulder before exiting the SUV.

The building that Tasha had dropped Ramone off at was just around the corner from Divine Boulevard, a mere three blocks from Holly House. It was a stone's throw from the span of woods that divided Meng's property and the abandoned resort. There weren't very many businesses in this part of the city, and like the resort, many of them had dried up long ago.

Maalik and I went several buildings down from the point where Tasha slipped through, pressing ourselves into the shadows and scanning for any sign of movement from around every corner. When we reached Divine Boulevard, we ran across in the darkness where the streetlights didn't reach and used the tree line as cover, watching the entrance of the building as Tasha approached.

My axe was heavy against my back, and the humidity was ten times worse in the woods, as if all the rainwater had run off the streets and pooled at the edges of the island. I swatted a bug away from my face and then mouthed a sarcastic *sorry* when Maalik glared at me.

Pale light from a neighboring building reflected off the studs in Tasha's ear as she pulled her hood back and knocked on the rusty door. It seemed like forever before someone finally answered. The chirping of the crickets invaded my ears, and I strained to hear the conversation she was having with the doorman. It didn't look promising.

Tasha threw her hands up into the air as the door began to close. She pushed it back open with her foot, yelling at the man and rubbing her fingers together in his face as if demanding to be paid.

The doorman snatched her arm and took a step out of the building, pushing her back. A patch of molting skin stretched down one side of his face and over his mouth and chin, looking almost like a beard trying to crawl its way up to his bald head. There were no whites to his eyes, just full black, gleaming in the darkness.

Maalik pulled the tracking compact out of his pocket and flipped it open. His bottom lip curled down into a scowl. "The soul is still inside. I say we move now."

As if she'd heard him, Tasha pulled the can of angelica mace out of her hoodie and emptied it in the doorman's face. The crickets became a whisper as the demon's screams filled the night.

Tasha sucker-punched him in the gut, following it up with an elbow to his spine as he doubled over. When he hit the sidewalk with a gurgling hiss, she climbed on top of him and pillaged through his pockets until she found a switchblade.

By the time Maalik and I had crossed the street, she was on her feet again, holding the blade out between us and the open door like a question mark. "So, who gets door number one?"

Maalik's eyes swirled with smoke, and his hands began to glow. "If you stab me in the back with that, I will melt your eyeballs out of your head. Understand?"

Tasha took a shaky breath and nodded as if she might have been considering that an option. Her wide eyes turned on me next.

I hefted my axe over my shoulder and gripped it with both hands. "I don't need a threat. You're going in after him."

She nodded and followed Maalik as he ducked inside. I hurried after them, my chest humming with premature triumph.

⚔

CHAPTER TWENTY-THREE

"In any dispute, each side thinks it's in the right
and the other side is demons."
—Steven Pinker

The building where Ramone was being kept had been gutted, leaving only a partial brick wall that divided the place into two large rooms. After a quick sweep, it made it easy to see what we were up against, or rather, what we *weren't* up against. Ramone and a dozen more souls were bound and gagged in the room along the rear of the building. Kevin and Abe smashed through the back door about the same time we found them.

"We heard someone scream," Kevin said, his eyes darting around the room as if he expected to find a dead body now that all was quiet again. My ears were still ringing.

Maalik knelt down beside Ramone and pulled the dirty rag out of his mouth.

"There were more," he rasped. "They left not long ago."

"Do you know where to?" I pulled my hunting knife out of my boot and used it to cut through the ropes around his wrists and ankles.

Ramone shook his head and licked his chapped lips. "They said something about a boat, though. They had the child soul with them."

"Shit." I turned the knife over to him, and he set to work freeing the other souls. "Why didn't they take the rest of you?"

"Guess they didn't have the room. The demon in charge said something about only taking the ones with buyers."

Maalik swore under his breath. "Where'd Tasha go?"

She'd held back when we approached Ramone and the souls, and now she was gone. Figured.

"I'm going to kill her," I said, turning back toward the front door in time to see her drag the moaning doorman inside by his feet. His head caught on the uneven threshold and bounced on the hardwood floor, leaving a sweaty trail through the dust as Tasha pulled him along.

When he was in far enough, she closed the door and straddled him again, pushing the tip of the switchblade under one of his bulging eyes. "I'm going to ask once, pretty please, that you tell us where the boat is."

The doorman's flakey skin looked less intimidating and more like an unfortunate ailment at this angle. The end of his shirt had bunched up under his armpits during Tasha's man-handling, exposing a catfish belly that hung past the waistband of his jeans. Tasha's knees pinned his elbows to the floor, and his flopping around stilled as the switchblade bit through his skin.

"You're too late." He tilted his head back, stretching the tendons in his neck until they looked as if they might snap.

Tasha pushed the blade in a little farther, causing the crease under his eye to pool with blood.

"The west coast. The west coast!" the demon wailed, squeezing his eyes shut. "They have a boat hidden in a cave under the ridge. It's leaving tonight."

"Thanks, precious." Tasha smacked his cheek and stood, wiping the switchblade against her thigh.

"Abe, call in the Guard and take this one to the station," Maalik ordered, his voice dropping an octave as the hellfire stirred in his eyes again. He nodded to me, Tasha, and Kevin. "The rest of you, with me."

Outside, he pointed east down Divine Boulevard. "Lana and Kevin, take the travel booth. It'll be faster. We'll meet you there." He scooped up Tasha, cradling her against his chest as he kept a wary eye on her switchblade, and then took flight, heading west over of the city and toward the coast.

Kevin and I didn't waste any time. We took off down the street, leaping over the small stream that trickled along the curb as we moved up onto the sidewalk. My heart pounded in my ears, and my axe felt as if it were trying to beat its way through the center of my back as I ran.

We slammed into the booth at full speed. My hands shook as I inserted a coin, and I almost selected the wrong stop. Kevin gave me a relieved look when the right destination lit up the screen, and we were ejected onto Westwood Drive, right in front of Tasha's favorite grocery store.

"Come on." I went ahead of Kevin, running past the building and into the woods. Maalik's wings whooshed through the air above. It was too dark to tell exactly where, but I pressed on without waiting to see. Jai Ling was somewhere ahead, along with whoever was responsible and in need of a beating.

Saplings groped and snagged at me as I worked my way through the undergrowth. It seemed thicker than before, but maybe that was just my body aching from rushing around the city. Something snapped, and Kevin groaned behind me. A second later, I heard him moving again. The woods were unkind, especially in the dark.

In the distance, the sound of water slapped against a boat hull, and it motivated me to move faster. I used my axe to clear a path until I reached the edge of the woods where a ragged cliff stretched out over the sea. The gentle hush of the waves was soothing. It had a calming effect that seemed out of place, until a delicate song echoed across the water.

"Sirens." I gasped.

Kevin stepped through the woods behind me, his eyes growing wide as the song reached his ears. His fingers fumbled along the edge of his quiver, seeking out a hidden pocket that he retrieved a set of plugs from. He jammed them into his ears and swallowed hard, taking a deep breath before he nodded to signal that he was ready to go on.

We followed the lip of the cliff until we reached a shadowy clearing tucked under the canopy of several tall trees. Maalik and Tasha slipped out of the woods behind us, and I nearly screamed before realizing it was them. The pitch-black was unnerving, and only the soft glow of Maalik's eyes saved us from being consumed by it entirely.

Maalik pressed a finger to his lips and pointed over the edge of the ridge. I could hear voices. They were soft, almost indiscernible, but they soon became clearer. The slap of the water against a boat grew louder, too.

"Just a few more," someone said. "Tell Eurynome to get ready to open the passage."

The wind picked up along the ridge, and I shivered as it cooled the sweat on my skin. I couldn't seem to catch my breath.

"They've already loaded the boat, and they got the queen bee of the sea down there," Tasha whispered. "What are we supposed to do now?"

Part of me was surprised that she was still tagging along, trying to make herself useful. She'd done what the contract demanded of her, and if Jenni had been in a position to honor it, Tasha could have punched her ticket by now and called it a night.

Maalik's brow furrowed, and he sent a desperate look up at the sky before dragging his hands down his face.

"That thingamabob that Warren gave you," Kevin said, pointing at my wrist. "Isn't it supposed to suck up souls or something?"

I gave him a horrified look. "You are not seriously suggesting I try this thing out right now," I hissed.

"It's either that or we wait to see if the Guard can make it here in time before the sirens suck all those souls down the drain and off to the land of wherever."

Maalik blew out an anxious breath. "It's worth a shot. I'll drop you on the boat to do your—whatever." He nodded at the gauntlet as I rolled up my sleeve.

Kevin pulled an arrow from his quiver. "If they try to open a portal, I'll create a diversion."

"What about me?" Tasha asked, waving the switchblade around as if to remind us she had procured a weapon and had done us a favor by not slitting our throats with it.

Maalik's jaw flexed as uncertainty and raging impatience warped his features. "Find their trail through the woods and see if you can stall them from loading the remaining souls," he said. Then he scooped me up under the arms, not at all as gently as he'd handled Tasha, and yanked me into the air before anyone could protest the plan.

I wanted to remind him again that I was captain of this fancy new unit, however short-lived it might be, but the wind was crueler away from the shelter of the trees. It filled my mouth and nose, stealing my breath and fueling the panic I was already battling from being consumed by the absolute darkness. Up in the naked sky above the sea, there was nothing for the embers in Maalik's eyes to illuminate.

I didn't find relief until we dipped under the cliff. The wind whistled through the shallow cave, rocking a small ferryboat in the tide, its outline dimly lit by a lantern hanging from the balcony of the stern cabin. If it didn't depart soon, the roof of the boat would reach the underside of the cliff, and it would be trapped there while everyone inside died a slow, agonizing death.

I spotted a siren in the water, her green hair fanning out behind her, bleeding into the inky shadow of the sea. And then a second and a third appeared. They moved through the water like snakes, slithering just beneath the surface. I lost sight of them as Maalik and I touched down on the deck of the boat.

It was empty, and I had a despairing feeling that we'd just walked into a trap, until the hatch opened, and a barb-tailed demon crawled out. He didn't see us at first, giving us his back as he walked toward the opposite railing.

He was smaller than the doorman but better built, and his attire suggested that he was from a more privileged caste than the desperate, downtrodden circles the rebels liked to recruit from. The boat was probably his, and the doorman and everyone else was likely on his payroll. If the ghost market had a top dog, my money was on him.

"All set," he called to the sirens in the water. "Anchors aweigh."

The boat rocked suddenly, and I was thrown forward, my axe clanking against the deck floor. Maalik was saved by his wings, lifting a few feet in the air rather than kissing the deck like I had.

"Check below. I'll take care of this one," he said as the demon spun around to face us, hissing and spitting his surprise.

The barbed tail seemed like child's play now. The thing had three mouths and an overgrowth of eyes that consumed the headspace where most would expect to find hair. I was more than happy to let Maalik have him.

I grabbed my axe and crawled across the deck on my hands and knees as the boat pitched again, causing me to slide across the slick boards and to the hatch as if it were home plate. I fell through, feet first, missed the ladder entirely, and landed on my side with an undignified *oomph*.

Twenty souls were chained around the inside cabin wall. The shackles were medieval as if they'd been salvaged from a castle dungeon. The fact that I wouldn't be able to cut them free with my axe sent a wave of dread through me, but then I remembered Warren's soul gauntlet. Maybe I wouldn't have to get my lumberjack on, after all. There was only one way to find out.

I rushed over to the nearest soul and held up the gauntlet, trying to decide if it mattered where I positioned the thing. The pamphlet hadn't shown a diagram. I'd have to put that down in my notes for Warren. In the meantime, I opted for trial and error, pressing the dome on the cuff to the soul's shoulder. When nothing extraordinary happened immediately, I moved the dome around, rubbing it over his face and chest.

The soul's patience wasn't much better than my own. His mouth twisted with annoyance, as if having me feel him up was somehow worse than being chained to the wall. Before he could say anything, the gauntlet whirred to life, and the soul turned a pale shade of blue. His features blurred, dissolving into a cloud of shrinking soul matter that was quickly sucked inside the dome.

"Aha!" I cheered triumphantly, while the remaining souls exploded into full-blown hysteria. "It's okay," I shouted. "I'm one of the good guys. Really." My disclaimer was poorly timed, and no one seemed to hear it.

I vowed to be more considerate in the future and moved on to the next soul, not wanting to be caught on the boat when Eurynome and her minions decided it was time to split. I only paused once when I came across Jai Ling tucked away in the far corner. She was the only soul who didn't scream in my face.

"Is Meng okay?" she asked, completely ignoring her own predicament.

I grinned and kissed the top of her head. "She will be now." I touched the dome of the gauntlet to her arm.

The gauntlet grew heavier and hotter with each soul it consumed, and I remembered the eight-soul capacity warning only after I'd snapped up all twenty in the cabin. I was imagining Warren's surprise at that revelation when a loud thump sounded on the deck above. I wondered how Maalik was faring and decided maybe it was time to lend him a hand with Captain Eyeballs.

As I climbed up the ladder to the hatch, an arrow whistled past my cheek and stuck in the deck floor a few feet ahead. I glanced up to find the culprit and realized that the boat had made it out past the ridge. Two nephilim guards hovered above the tree line. They manned a spotlight as wide around as a hula hoop, aiming it at the boat's deck where I had just emerged. My eyes watered, and I lifted a hand to shield my face from the blinding light.

Kevin waved to me from the peak of a cliff, his bow in his other hand. "Sorry," he shouted before stringing another arrow.

I huffed and hooked my axe on the hatch opening, using it to pull myself the rest of the way out. The gauntlet felt like a lead weight, and my shoulder pinched whenever I allowed my hand to rest at my side.

"Maalik?" I leaned over the deck railing and scanned the water for the sirens.

The boat was spinning, making me dizzy as it turned faster and faster. The spotlight flickered across my vision, blurring until I began to wonder if maybe I was at a rave and someone had slipped something in my drink. Was any of this real?

"Maalik!" I shouted and clutched my axe to my chest, grasping the railing with the hand rendered feeble by the gauntlet.

The stern of the boat tipped up in the air, and the bow dipped into the sea where a whirlpool had begun to form. Eurynome, the golden-tailed mermaid goddess and former rebel general, rose out of the funnel's depths. Her pale hands beckoned the boat closer as if pulling it along by an invisible rope.

My legs trembled, but I did my best to stay upright against the steep incline. I tucked one foot between a pair of spindles along the railing and twisted my body, throwing my axe in a wild arc at the deck floor that was quickly tilting up into a wall at my back. My blade wedged between two boards, offering meager leverage that I already knew wouldn't last.

Eurynome's eyes met mine, and she smiled wickedly. "Come along, little reaper. I'm sure we can sell you, too."

My stomach churned, and I couldn't find my next breath. Everything bled together until all I could make out was Eurynome's Cheshire Cat grin and the distorted planks bending at an awkward angle toward the water.

CHAPTER TWENTY-FOUR

"The only way to deal with an unfree world is to become so absolutely free that your very existence is an act of rebellion."
—*Albert Camus*

The sea rose slowly around me as Eurynome pulled the boat deeper into the whirlpool, and just when I thought we'd passed the point of no return, a flaming arrow hissed through the air, sinking perfectly in the pit of Eurynome's throat. The boat jerked, tipping upright violently.

I tried to hold tight to my axe, but the deck floor splintered as the blade tore free, the handle ripping from my fingers with bruising force. I was flung out over the water, away from the glow of the spotlight and into the shadows, where I was sure the sirens waited to drown me.

Suspended over the sea, holding my breath and waiting to meet my watery end, I had a few final thoughts. They weren't very coherent or organized, but that hardly seemed to matter at this point.

The first of these was that Kevin was one hell of a shot. I was quite proud of him, and I was sorry that I wouldn't get the chance to express that more eloquently, his intimacy issues be damned.

My second thought was that I had no less than twenty high-priority souls attached to my wrist, including Jai Ling. Maybe the Guard could drag the coast and retrieve the gauntlet in the morning. I was pretty sure the three-hour maximum was as modest a guesstimate as the eight-soul capacity.

My hand felt like it was made of titanium and on fire. If there was a silver lining to be had in this moment, it was that the sea might just be cold enough to provide a sliver of relief before I up and died.

A third thought was on its way to me when a loud buzzing filled my ears. A swarm of flies circled my body, and I felt the sea spray my cheek. My fingers broke the surface for a second as the flies struggled to lift me away from the water. They concentrated themselves across my back and under my knees, and as the ridge came into view beneath us, Bub materialized, cradling me in his arms.

He set me down on the ledge with a strained grunt and gasped to find his next breath. "What have I been feeding you?"

"It's this, not my ass," I said, clumsily holding up my numb hand and the gauntlet.

Bub stared at me a moment, his amusement at our post-near-death conversation lighting his face. "Ready to skip town yet, love?"

"I want my cookie first," I said, only half teasing.

A soft laugh whispered past his lips, and then he tilted his ear up as if he could hear something I couldn't. "I don't have a cookie, but my tiny troops did retrieve this."

Something sparkled in the dark, reflecting the traces of light that slipped through the trees as the Nephilim Guard filled the ridge farther up from our little nook. The buzzing swarm parted before me, revealing my axe.

It was better than a cookie. I looped the strap over my shoulder and wobbled against the uneven weight of the axe, grinning even though I felt like I'd just had my ass kicked six ways to Sunday.

Someone shouted my name, and Bub snuck a kiss before taking wing again, dissolving into his swarm and scattering through the dark woods behind me.

"I'm here," I yelled to the guards fluttering overhead.

Abe dropped down through the treetops and led me out of the woods to the clearing where the Guard had gathered up the demons in league with Eurynome, including the extra mouthy one Maalik had tangled with on the boat.

Several sirens floated face down in the sea, arrows sticking out of their backs and blood staining the water around them like tar. It was a gruesome sight, and I imagined a necessary outcome after Eurynome bit the big one. Kevin's steady bow was probably the only reason the Guard hadn't been sung off the cliff en masse.

An uproar on land drew my attention back to the ridge. Two nephilim guards dragged Tasha away while Jenni watched impassively.

"I have immunity!" Tasha shrieked. Her wild eyes found me, and she thrashed against the guards. "Tell them. Tell them, Lana!"

I shivered and went to stand beside Jenni. I'd known the contract was a joke, but I hadn't really expected the punchline to come so soon. The shock of it sent a jolt of guilt through me, but what could I do that wouldn't put me in the cell next to Tasha's?

"Where's Maalik?" I asked as we watched Tasha and the guards disappear through the trees, heading back into the city.

"Meng's." Jenni sighed. "He broke a wing."

"Well, I guess I can forgive him then."

"How'd you manage to get off that boat? I didn't see any guards out that far." Jenni gave me a knowing frown.

I avoided her question by pressing the little button on the inside edge of the gauntlet, and the outer dome sprang open. The dial inside had melted, filling the cartoony meter with skunky, black plastic. Warren was going to kill me. I tried to remember how the thing worked and was rewarded with a squeal from one of the guards when I managed to press the right lever inside the gadget.

Blue soul matter spilled out of the smoking dome, dropping into puddles at my feet. They grew, spreading out across the ridge as they stretched and formed into humanoid shapes, slowly reclaiming their features until they were whole again.

Jenni's eyes latched onto the gauntlet. I could see her wheels turning. The device's potential for general harvesting wasn't lost on me either. The future of Reapers Inc. was about to get interesting.

As the souls reoriented themselves, the Nephilim Guard made the rounds and checked them against their database. I was too tired to math, but I didn't need a headcount to know this wasn't everyone on the list. For starters, I hadn't come across Ruth Summerdale.

"What's going to happen to Tasha?" I asked Jenni.

"That's up to the council now."

I chewed my bottom lip. "She followed through on her end of the deal. Went above and beyond, actually."

Jenni gave me a tired smile. "Go home, Lana. It's late, and you have a meeting with the council tomorrow afternoon."

I shuddered and tucked my aching hand against my stomach as I turned to gape at her. "They're not *really* going to go through with this ruling bullshit after tonight, are they?"

Jenni pressed her lips together, her smile looking less reassuring. "Go home," she repeated. "Get some sleep. We'll sort all of this out tomorrow."

I left the ridge and followed the path the guards had tromped through the woods, thinking maybe Tasha wasn't the only one who had been screwed. At least she was going down kicking and screaming.

"Wait up!" Kevin cut through the woods and ran to join me. "What happened to Maalik and Tasha?"

My shoulders squared. Explaining the backstabbing scheme to my apprentice hadn't been part of the plan. "Maalik is at Meng's. Something took a bite out of him," I said, hoping that would buy some time while I figured out what to say about Tasha.

"I saw! It was pretty amazing. Maalik had that demon by the tail, like, actually *by* the *tail*." Kevin's breath hitched as he skipped along beside me. "He lit him up like a sparkler, but the guy jumped on his back and tried to rip his wings off.

That's when the Guard showed up, and the sea went all spin cycle. I lost sight of the battle when I moved to find higher ground. My arrows couldn't reach where the boat had drifted out to."

"Great shooting, by the way." I slapped his back and then wrapped my arm around his shoulders, giving him a squeeze.

Kevin's face flushed. "I almost hit you."

"Yeah, but you *did* hit Eurynome, thereby saving my ass, thereby earning my forgiveness, no apology needed."

"Where's Tasha?" he asked again, scanning the grocery store parking lot as we exited the woods.

I sighed and looked down at the gauntlet on my wrist. It felt lighter now, like aluminum foil, and I had a hard time believing that it was the same burning weight I'd endured just a few moments before.

Kevin glanced over his shoulder, back toward the trail parting the woods. "Did she survive the battle?"

"I don't know yet." I crossed Westwood Drive and entered the travel booth on the corner, slipping a coin in the dash as Kevin joined me. The perplexed look hadn't left his face, but he didn't ask any more questions.

The booth glass went opaque, lights streaking through it in some mathematical, black magic sequence. When it cleared, Holly House waited across the street. A beam of fluorescent light stretched out across the front garden, coming from the parking garage, where Warren waited. His wings twitched nervously as I crossed the lawn.

"I'll see you upstairs," Kevin said, waving to Warren before he punched in his code at the front door.

"Well?" Warren asked eagerly, rubbing his hands together as he eyeballed the gauntlet.

"I can't get it off." I held my hand out to him, giving it a shake when he didn't move as fast as I wanted him to. My wrist was itching something fierce.

Warren fingered along the outer rim of the cuff, pinching my skin a time or two before he finally found the release button. The gauntlet popped open with an audible click, exposing my blistered flesh underneath. I glared at Warren as he blubbered apologetically.

"I'll add a layer of insulating foam to future models for more comfortable wear," he said, turning the gauntlet over in his hand to inspect the soul dome. When the meter cover popped open, he gasped at the melted inner workings.

"Might want to consider more durable parts, too." I gave him a sheepish smile.

"You overheated it." He poked at the hardened plastic and gave me a callous look. "How many souls did you hold in here?"

I rolled my eyes. "It wasn't that many."

"Lana?"

"Twenty." I cradled my injured wrist, hoping a little sympathy would soften the blow. "I had to."

Warren's eyes bulged. "My greatest invention, my masterpiece, and you had to go and botch it by not following the safety guidelines."

"Sorry," I mumbled. "You asked me to test it in the field."

Warren tsked and walked away from me toward his work-shop tucked in the back corner of the garage. "Guess I learned my lesson."

"You're welcome." I huffed and hefted my axe up higher on my shoulder before entering the lobby through the garage entrance.

Charlie glanced up from the front desk as I headed for the elevators. He pressed his lips together and looked back down at his desk without a hello. His friendliness had expired about the same time Holly's had, but I'd ignored it for the most part.

My tolerance threshold just wasn't up for it tonight. I curled back around and stopped in front of him, slapping my good hand down on the counter.

Charlie looked up with a sour expression. "Can I help you?"

"Yes, you can," I said with forced cheer. "I'd like to submit my thirty-day move-out notice. Do you keep those forms down here, or does Holly have them stashed in a nest somewhere?"

Charlie's wings bristled, but he opened a drawer and pulled out a sheet of paper. He gave it a quick glance and then slid it across the counter to me. When I reached for it, he held on until I looked at him.

"You won't find a decent place in the city without Holly's endorsement. You realize that, don't you?" He almost looked sorry for me.

I snatched the page out of his hand and smiled. "Who says I'm going to live in the city?"

CHAPTER TWENTY-FIVE

"Many that live deserve death. And some that die deserve life. Can you give it to them? Then do not be too eager to deal out death in judgement. For even the very wise cannot see all ends."
—J. R. R. Tolkien

On a scale of one to *fuck my life*, I'd been hanging around a solid eight for the past few days. It seemed so incredibly unfair that I would have to go through the trouble of saving a bunch of fancy souls and bringing down the soul-traffickers responsible just to turn around and face uncertain judgment from a bunch of jerks who thought they were better than me.

It wasn't lost on me that Tasha was facing down that same demon. But I had good reasons for the actions I was being reprimanded for. Did she? I really wasn't sure now, and I felt like every bit the jerk Ridwan was for not bothering to ask.

My mind kept circling back to her while I prepared for my meeting with the council Wednesday afternoon. I shuffled around the condo like a zombie, digging through my closet in a quest to find something that invoked innocence. I discovered a blue blouse and held it over my chest in front of the mirror on my dresser.

Bub stepped in behind me, placing a kiss on my bare shoulder. "Is that what I'll be tearing off of you later tonight, my love?"

I sighed. "Maybe I should wear black. It's only appropriate for a funeral."

"Stop that." Bub turned me around and lifted my wrapped hand to his lips for a kiss. Then he tucked a rolled-up piece of parchment in my fingers. "I know you have Morgan's tricky necklace somewhere around here, and now you have an incantation slip to open a portal into the mortal realm." He tilted his head from side to side with a frown. "Ideally, if it comes right down to it, I'd prefer we use that to squeeze the houseboat through to the other side. That would be much preferred to having to scrounge about among the humans until we've gathered our bearings."

I grinned. "Do you even know how to scrounge?"

"No, but I'm quite effective at possession, being the prince of demons and all." He wagged his eyebrows. Then his face turned serious. "I'll await your call at the manor. If the verdict is an unpleasant one, and if you can get away without using the incantation, meet me at the houseboat on the Styx, and we'll be on our way."

"What if I do have to use the incantation?" I asked with a frown.

Bub shrugged. "Then meet me at the houseboat anyway. I'll have our things ready just in case, and we'll depart together to begin our new life as amateur scroungers."

A nervous thrill shot through me. Could we really do this? Just run away and never return to Limbo City? It hurt to think on it for too long, and I really hadn't until now.

"The hounds—" I began, glancing over to where they napped on the bed.

"The pups are plenty big enough now to part from their mother. I'll bring Saul and Coreen with me to Tartarus."

My forehead throbbed as I thought of Kevin and how betrayed he would feel. Would he understand? Would Gabriel? Would Naledi be able to track us down and bring us to justice, being connected to the very glue that held both worlds together? Would she do that on the council's behalf?

My chest ached as I thought of all the things I would have to leave behind, all the places I'd never be able to see again. After everything, was this really what it all came down to?

Bub reached down into the black jewelry box on my dresser and pulled out the crystal bands Kevin had tracked down for me. He held them up against the blue blouse still draped over my chest. "You should wear these. You'll look like a princess, and what sort of heathen would sentence a princess to death?"

"What sort of angel, you mean," I grumbled under my breath as I stepped into the closet to change.

The day had slipped away too soon, and I hated that I couldn't give those I cared about a proper goodbye. It would be too risky, and there was the voice in the back of my head that kept insisting it wasn't necessary. Everything was going to be fine. That voice had been progressively shrinking, but it was still there, and it held fast to the only bit of sanity I had left.

The only goodbyes I could manage without alerting the world were to the helljack puppies. I gave them each a full-body scratch and smooshed their slobbery faces in my hands so I could kiss the spot between their ears without having them lick my makeup off.

Kevin watched the interaction from the front door, holding a lead in each hand. "Jesus, Lana. I'm just taking them for a walk."

"I know." I picked at the puppy hair clinging to my slacks. "Just needed a little good luck for my debriefing with the council." I didn't have the heart to tell him what the meeting was really about.

"I still don't see why Jenni can't do that." He looked annoyed on my behalf, though not for long when I surprised him with a hug.

"Can never be too lucky," I said as he pulled away with a startled look.

"Okay, then. See you later." He clipped on the helljacks' leads and left before me, blinking stiffly and shaking his head.

Gabriel wouldn't have thought twice about me hugging him, but Holly had sent him off on some menial cherub task for the Board of Heavenly Hosts. I was pretty sure it was an attempt to keep him occupied while they dealt with me. That was a comforting thought.

When I left the condo to head to Reapers Inc., I found Abe waiting for me in the lobby. He was back in his standard-issue armor, but the look on his face said he wasn't too happy about it. His cheeks colored with shame as he approached me. "I'm here on the council's orders," he said under his breath, sending Charlie an unfriendly glance over his shoulder.

I nodded. "I figured as much. Don't sweat it. I'm not making a run for it or anything."

"Are you sure?" he whispered. "Because it would be their own fault for sending a guard who's already lost you once before."

I grinned. "It's okay, Abe."

He took a deep breath and nodded. "All right, then. But just so you know, if you change your mind, I didn't see anything."

"I appreciate that," I said as we crossed the lobby and headed outside.

We took the travel booths through the city, and Abe and I walked inside Reapers Inc. together. Ross spotted us in the lobby and called Abe over, leaving me to ride up in an elevator by myself. I guess they figured if I'd made it this far without a fight, I was here to stay.

My heart hammered away as the elevator ascended. I could feel the thrum of my pulse pushing against my temples, and my breath was much too labored. If I didn't get it under control soon, I was going to hyperventilate.

The elevator jolted as it came to a stop on the thirty-seventh floor. From Jenni's curt attitude, I hadn't expected another pre-meeting. My bubble of hope was popped when I found Naledi waiting for me instead.

"Not a word," she whispered, stepping into the elevator beside me. She pushed the button for the seventy-third floor, and the car began to move again.

I opened my mouth to ask what she was doing on the torture level, but she cut me off. "Remember those special coins Winston designed to take you to the throne realm from anywhere?"

"The ones the council deemed illegal?"

"Yes." She gave me a pointed look. "He also had one he liked to use to go wherever he pleased, even after the travel booths went into effect. Looked just like the regular coins with Cernunnos' stag emblem and everything."

"Sounds like Winston." I smiled sadly, remembering all of his shenanigans.

"You're going to need it," Naledi said. She bumped her shoulder against mine, and I felt a weight drop into the pocket of my slacks.

At the same time, a weight dropped on my heart. Naledi had visions of the future. If she'd seen something that made her believe I would need a speedy escape route today, then this whole meeting was a pointless waste of time.

The ghost market had been taken down, and I should have been proud of that accomplishment, but I could already see the ways Ridwan would likely try to discredit me. Not all of the missing souls had been accounted for, and Maalik had taken charge of the mission in the end. Even if that fact weren't revealed, his broken wing would reveal his involvement at the very least.

The elevator dinged as we reached the council floor, and I fumbled for the down button. Naledi's hand snatched mine, and she shook her head as the doors slid open.

"Not yet," she whispered. "You'll know when it's time."

I swallowed and ran a hand over my forehead, wiping away the sweat that had begun to bead across my brow.

Parvati exited the conference room at the end of the hallway and waved her two left arms, luring us closer. Her smile was warm and inviting, and I wondered if she already knew what was to become of me.

"Good afternoon," she said sweetly, directing us inside the room and to a pair of open seats.

I scanned the room and found Maalik. His right wing was bandaged and folded in against his back at an awkward angle. The circles under his eyes made me wonder if he'd slept at all since the battle on the sea, and when his gaze met mine, a wave of hopeless despair settled in my stomach. He was prepared to watch me die today. He'd already convinced himself there was nothing he could do to change that.

"What is the soul doing here?" Ridwan said, reclining in a chair at the end of the table. "We have not approved a new committee as of yet. She has no vote."

"She's not here to vote," Jenni said. She sat at the opposite end of the table, her index and middle fingers rubbing one temple as she glared at the angel. "She's here to witness, as the soul on the Throne of Eternity, which is her right."

Ridwan snorted and his wings fluttered against the back of his leather seat.

I took a long look around the table, trying to translate all the different expressions. Holly and Cindy had a self-righteous air about them. Typical. Their smugness contrasted with Meng Po's weathered smile. She waved to me from her corner of the table.

"Jai Ling prays to the ancestors for you today," she said.

I swallowed and nodded my thanks, letting my eyes move on to Kwan Yin. Her statuesque face revealed nothing new, which made the Green Man's wild grin all the more alarming.

"I call first order of business," he said, sitting up tall in his chair.

Ridwan slammed his fist on the table. "We already have a first order of business."

"I called it first, so you'll have to wait," the Green Man insisted.

"Get on with it then," Ridwan said through clenched teeth. His face was swollen with rage as if the idea of me living for five minutes longer vexed him beyond all reason.

The Green Man cleared his throat and folded his hands over the table. "The negotiation of the century has concluded with a beneficial outcome for all. The Sphinx Congress has been disbanded. Their seat and territory have been surrendered to the authority of the Summerland Society."

"Now wait just one minute." Ridwan stood, pushing his chair back and into the wall. "You haven't approved any of this with the council—"

The ivy stretched across the Green Man's chest tightened as he took a deep breath. "You are still new to this council, so we will pardon your ignorance of negotiations that began decades before your arrival. However, your ignorance of sub-committee structure is a bit disappointing."

Ridwan began turning colors again, but Maalik spoke first. "Please, brother. A shouting match will not change the truth he speaks."

Parvati nodded in agreement. "As long as a subcommittee does not exceed three seats on the council, they are free to merge and divide as they see fit."

Ridwan breathed in through his nose and pulled his chair back to the table. "It does not matter what committee Horus is on. He is still suspended from the council until his hearing."

The Green Man's smile broadened. "Horus has resigned from the council. Athena will be taking his place." He clapped his hands, and the conference room door opened.

The goddess of wisdom and weaving stepped inside, drawing a series of surprised gasps. Her eyes scanned the room, lighting playfully when they found me. She took an empty chair and smiled blankly at Ridwan as his face twisted again. I wondered if it was possible for an angel to have a stroke.

"Now," the Green Man said, turning back to Ridwan. "Do you have a second order of business you'd like to pro-pose?"

CHAPTER TWENTY-SIX

"Everyone suffers some injustice in life, and what better motiva-
tion than to help others not suffer in the same way."
—Bella Thorne

I dry heaved over the sink in the tiny bathroom off the lobby. I thought I'd make it home to have my meltdown in peace, but things just hadn't worked out that way.

I was alive by the grace of one vote.

I was never shopping anywhere but at Athena's again. I would set up a shrine to her in the living room of the new manor. If Bub and I were able to make babies, I would have named them all after her.

My manic joy was only staled by the fact that Tasha was next. And she didn't have the allies I'd made. But what could I do? I thought of the guilt-stricken expression Maalik had worn in the meeting, and then caught sight of myself in the mirror and realized that I wore that same hopeless, all-is-lost look. Pathetic.

I pressed my back against the closed bathroom door and slid down to the floor, gasping when the coin in my pocket clanked against the tile through the material of my pants.

Naledi had been wrong. How was that even possible? It sent a shadow of doubt through me. Would Ridwan demand a second vote? Would Athena change her mind? Why would Naledi think I'd need it if the vote were going to be in my favor?

You'll know when it's time.

I pulled the coin out of my pocket, along with the incantation slip Bub had given me. Morgan's stone necklace was cool against my chest, hanging hidden beneath my blouse. I fingered it through the thin material, giving it a twist and fading from sight.

I was pretty sure this was a terrible idea. But I was also sure that it was the only way I'd be able to live with myself.

I stuffed the coin and incantation back into my pocket before I left the bathroom. Then I followed a dinner cart into an elevator and rode with it up to the seventieth floor.

Tasha had been right. They only seemed to serve bread and bean soup to the prisoners. I followed the cart down the hallway to her cell, trying to stay a safe distance back in case my nervous mouth-breathing alerted the waiter.

The nephilim delivered Tack's meal first, giving me a few precious seconds alone with the cart. I took the coin and the incantation out of my pocket and fingered open the roll on Tasha's tray, shoving the items inside as far as I could without mashing the bread too badly. Then I stepped out of the waiter's path as he came out of Tack's room.

He took Tasha's meal and approached her door with more caution, unlocking the small slot under the window and shoving the tray through as quickly as possible. When the platter and food smashed against the window, raining bean soup down the glass, I understood why.

"Ungrateful bitch," the nephilim mumbled as he wheeled the cart away.

I waited until he'd disappeared before tapping softly at the window, straining to see Tasha through the fog of bean goop. "Tasha," I hissed. "Come on, I don't have a lot of time."

Fingers wiped through the mess on the window, and Tasha's angry eyes glared right through me. "Who's there?"

"It's Lana," I whispered.

"What the hell do you want?"

"You need to get out of here."

"You think?" She rolled her eyes and rubbed at the glass some more, moving around to see if she could catch a glimpse of me.

"The bread. Find the bread the waiter just brought you."

"What the fuck kind of joke is this?" She glanced down at the floor around her feet for a minute, as if she was sure I was just screwing with her for the fun of it, but then she found the roll and held it up to the window. "What now? Should I turn in three circles or click my heels maybe?"

"There's a skeleton coin in there that will get you out of that cell, and an incantation slip that will get your yacht over to the mortal sea."

Tasha paled and shook her head. "Fuck that yacht. I'm not trying that again."

I remembered the scar I'd seen on her back. "Don't worry. That's what the bread is for."

"Right." Tasha scoffed and hugged herself.

"Trust me," I said.

"Why the hell would I do that?" She glared through the glass again, trying to see me. "You fucked me over. I was supposed to have immunity. Tack, too."

"I know. I'm sorry." I swallowed and bit my bottom lip. "Look, I'm trying to make things right. It's not like you really wanted to go back to work as a reaper again, did you?"

She rolled her eyes. "It didn't exactly sound like buckets of fun, but it would have definitely been a fate better than death."

"That doesn't have to be your fate, Tasha."

She thought it over for a minute and then held the roll up to the window, figuring I could see her even if she couldn't see me. "Thanks, precious. This is one hell of a last meal."

CHAPTER TWENTY-SEVEN

"Everything I did in my life that was
worthwhile, I caught hell for."
—*Earl Warren*

The chicken Bub had prepared for our celebratory dinner was amazing. So amazing, in fact, that Kevin had invited himself to join us. And then Gabriel returned from wherever Holly had sent him off to and decided to stick around for a bite too, claiming that eating food prepared by my demon consort was a crucial step in their budding friendship. I let him win that argument.

The dinner conversation spilled over into dessert—one of my famous apple pies—and then we cracked open a few Ambrosia Ales and riffled through my John Wayne collection. I'd expected Bub to pout about our *second* dessert being delayed, but he seemed just as amused as I was by Gabriel finally warming up to him.

We were all sprawled across the couches in the living room, watching *Pals of the Saddle*, when someone tried to put their fist through the front door.

"I know it was you," a wrathful voice yelled.

Saul's head snapped up with a growl, and Coreen curled herself more tightly around the helljack puppies. Gabriel made it to the door first, and Bub was a step behind him.

Ridwan stood in the hallway, his wings extended, and his chest puffed out. His bloodshot eyes glared past Gabriel and Bub, seeking me out.

"I know it was you," he said again.

It was hard to play innocent when he looked as if he were prepared to take the whole building down to get to me, but I at least managed to contain my gloating. "What was me?"

"You freed that traitor and her demon sidekick." His eyes darted from me to Bub, and he scoffed as if he saw a resemblance to Tasha and Tack.

Gabriel scratched his head. "I thought Maalik said she was wearing a tracking bracelet."

Ridwan's lips peeled back to bare his clenched teeth. "It was removed after the battle. How convenient." He held a finger up in the air. "The Nephilim Guard will find them, and when they do, I'll be able to prove it was your doing."

"Lana's been here with us all evening," Gabriel said.

Bub nodded. "She came home right after the hearing and baked the most sinfully delicious apple pie."

Kevin hadn't moved from the couch, but he piped up long enough to vouch for me, too. "À la mode," he added, nodding enthusiastically.

Ridwan snarled. He reeled his fist back and slammed it against the doorframe in a fit of rage.

Gabriel's mouth gaped open. "I wouldn't do that—"

But his warning came too late. The Latin prayers engraved in the woodwork flared to life, sending a line of blue fire up Ridwan's arm. It burned through the sleeve of his robe until it reached his wing, where it promptly ignited as if the angel had recently bathed in gasoline.

He screamed and flapped his arm and wing about, setting fire to a lampshade on a side table in the hallway.

"Bloody hell." Bub sighed and grabbed the fire extinguisher from under the kitchen sink. He ran out into the hallway and sprayed foam over Ridwan, taking special care not to miss his face, which burned even brighter than the fire had.

The angel sputtered and stumbled down the hallway toward the elevator. He took a ragged breath as he turned around, pointing a finger at me as he pounded his fist against the down button.

"I will see you hang if it's the last thing I accomplish on this council," he said. "Your kind is a curse on Eternity, and I'm here to break it. They will all see you for what you are soon enough." The elevator dinged open, and he swooped inside, shedding singed feathers as he fled.

Gabriel watched with a comical expression, his lips pinched together in a tight line that his grin was slowly overpowering. A laugh bubbled up from his chest, but he tried to disguise it with a cough.

Bub waved the hose of the extinguisher at Ridwan. "You're welcome!" He huffed out an exasperated sigh. "We demon sidekicks are so underappreciated."

Ridwan fumed at us as the doors of the elevator slid shut, sealing away his hateful face.

"Those wings are going to be fun to explain at the board meeting tomorrow morning." Gabriel looked at me and snorted. "I'm totally going to tell everyone the Lord of the Flies saved his sorry ass."

Bub waited for Gabriel to turn around and head back to the living room before he leaned down to kiss the side of my neck. "You naughty, naughty girl."

I grinned and looked up at him from under my lashes. "I'm sure I have no idea what you're talking about."

Catch up with Lana and company in…

HELLFIRE AND BRIMSTONE

LANA HARVEY, REAPERS INC. BOOK SEVEN

Available Now in Print, eBook, and Audio!

The end is nigh...

Lana Harvey is on top of the world—the underworld, that is. With the war fallout tapering off, she finds herself reduced back to mundane soul harvesting. It's not a fancy gig, and the pay isn't thrilling, but that hardly matters now that she's shacking up with her retired demon consort, Beelzebub.

The afterlives have stabilized, and all seems well, until an average day on the job crosses Lana's path with not one but two ghosts she thought were long gone. The startling revelation rips open old wounds and sends her on a quest to discover the truth behind her mentor's mysterious death, and what it could mean for the fate of Eternity.

ACKNOWLEDGMENTS

2019 10-year anniversary update: I can hardly believe that Lana turns 10 this year! To celebrate, I asked Rebecca Frank to revamp the cover designs, my cousin Kaitlyn Beck to pose as Lana, my husband Paul to photograph her, and my editor Chelle Olson to clean up my early work that I heavily relied on English-savvy teacher pals to proofread back in the day. I also can't forget shout-outs to Hollie Jackson, the epic narrator who voices Lana in the audiobooks; the Four Horsemen of the Bookocalypse, my amazing critique group; and THE professor George Shelley, whose enthusiasm for Lana's world motivated me at times I'd almost given up on writing. All my gratitude to you wonderful mavens who make my books shine and my heart swell.

Original acknowledgments: Six books and three short stories later, and I have a whole new appreciation for writers who tackle series work. Keeping all of one's fictitious facts straight is no easy feat. I know I've slipped up a time or two, accidentally swapped minor characters names, placed a business on the wrong street corner of Limbo City, but luckily, I have some really awesome editors and readers who let me know when they spot these inconsistencies. All remaining errors are my own.

I also owe a huge thanks to the usual suspects: my critique group the Four Horsemen of the Bookocalypse, THE Professor George Shelley, my saintly husband who takes care of all the things (including me) while I write, Andrea Cook who cheers me on with her Twitter release day countdowns. Then there's Angie Hacket, Robin Phillips, Kelly Byrd, Rachel Dawson, Lester Smith, and—ah hell, I could fill a whole book with the names of people who have encouraged and inspired me. But since I'm all out of time and space, please feel free to you add your name to that list right here:

Thank you from the bottom of my heart. For your sweet emails, your thoughtful reviews, or for just taking another stroll through Limbo City with me and Lana. I hope you'll join us again, one last time for book 7, *Hellfire and Brimstone*. xoxo

ABOUT THE AUTHOR

USA Today bestselling author **Angela Roquet** is a delightfully macabre weirdo. She lives in Missouri with her irresistible BFF husband, their sweet, clever son, and a majestic marshmallow of a Great Pyrenees in a house stuffed with books, toys, skulls, owls, and glitter-speckled craft supplies.

Angela is a member of the Science Fiction and Fantasy Writers Association, as well as the Four Horsemen of the Bookocalypse, her epic book critique group, where she's known as Death. When not swearing at the keyboard, she enjoys playing with her family and reading books that raise eyebrows.

You can find Angela online at **www.angelaroquet.com**

If you enjoyed this book, please leave a review or tell a friend. Your enthusiasm and support make these books possible, and it means the world to me!

www.ingramcontent.com/pod-product-compliance
Lightning Source LLC
Chambersburg PA
CBHW050846190726
48286CB00007B/2245